P9-BYZ-779

# A LONDON
# SCRAPBOOK

For: Harriett
with much love and
a life time of memory.
as ever,
Pal
July 08

Beaver's Pond Press

with much love and
of memory
...
...thank it
with much
a life that
is ever.

Tal
July 08

# A LONDON
# SCRAPBOOK

*at Way-*
*Place —*
*feb. 2001*

### A Memoir
## POLLY GROSE

Beaver's Pond Press

Also by Polly Grose:
*Thomas Janney, "Publisher of Truth"*
*Hannah*
*Phineas and His Cousins*

*A London Scrapbook* © copyright 2008 by Polly Grose. All rights reserved. No part of this book may be reproduced in any form whatsoever, by photography or xerography, or by any other means, by broadcast or transmission, by translation into any kind of language, nor by recording electronically or otherwise, without permission in writing from the author, except by a reviewer, who may quote brief passages in critical articles or reviews.

ISBN 13: 978-1-59298-233-2
ISBN 10: 1-59298-233-6
Library of Congress Catalog Number: 2008903454

Book design and typesetting: Jill Blumer
Printed in the United States of America

First Printing: 2008

12   11   10   09   08      5   4   3   2   1

**Beaver's Pond Press**

7104 Ohms Lane
Edina, Minnesota 55439 USA
(952) 829-8818
www.BeaversPondPress.com

To order, visit www.BookHouseFulfillment.com or call1-800-901-3480.
Reseller and special sales discounts available

DEDICATION

*For Charlie, Chris, and Michael*


ACKNOWLEDGMENTS

Everlasting thanks to Amy Friedman
for her inspired critique and expert editing.

And to Helen Kingman West
for our lively discussions of the memoir
and her lifelong friendship.

# Scrapbooks

Even on a humid August afternoon my fireplace glows, crackling with memories that burst from the vellum pages of our scrapbooks, David's and mine. Side by side, these specially bound books, tall and thick, stand touching each other within the polished teak case that nests inside the firebox. The chimney flue has been sealed. The fireplace, a sanctuary of memory, spits out the glowing embers of childhood, fragments of joy and sorrow, clues to secrets deeply buried, glimpses of lives well lived.

I close my eyes. I smell the salty air as David and I sail into the Solent from the Beaulieu River along the south coast of England or feel the afternoon breeze pick up and ruffle the Union Jack flying over the stern of our sloop as we leave the harbor at Porto Ercole. I see the raindrops running off our yellow oilskins. I hear the klaxon of the London taxi, touch the petals of the roses, daisies, and lilies of the Chelsea Green flower stall, the trays of sweets, aubergines, and melons in the markets of the Mediterranean towns, the markets David loved to photograph. I feel my husband's presence, a hint of his body aroma, a sort of basil, herby smell, rising from deep inside his chest. I taste the cool rosé wine from Bandol, remember discovering the path to the vineyard as we threaded our way though a mass of nude bathers sunning on the Med's rocky beach. I touch the wide-brimmed black straw hat I wore to the London wedding and feel his arm around my shoulder. Another hot August afternoon over fifteen years ago.

David taught me how to make a scrapbook, not to paste in every photograph from a trip; that's a photo album. A scrapbook maker selects and organizes his material around a theme. These books were David's personal accounts of his life over forty years, a social and political record of the time, with clippings from newspapers and magazines, cartoons, selected photographs of family, friends, and special mementoes. My husband preferred to photograph inanimate objects—statues, cemetery stones, and building porticos and facades, and, of course, boats and harbors—to photographing people. He used double-sided tape to secure each piece, under which he carefully noted the subject and date. In our London sitting room David lined up the books on special shelves from which he could easily pull down a volume when he needed to check a date or place. He spent time each day on his hobby, and as he grew older, and especially when he grew ill, he spent more and more time clipping and pasting. When the books became too heavy for him to lift from the shelf, I stood on a footstool to reach whichever volume he wished. He liked our team effort, and he encouraged me to pursue my own scrapbooking.

After David's death in 2002 I moved back from London to my Minneapolis roots, to a small condominium overlooking Lake Minnetonka in the western suburbs of Minneapolis. I added new bookshelves to house our large collection. But the scrapbooks, each one standing twenty-four by twelve inches, five inches across the back, over a hundred pages thick, were too tall and deep for ordinary shelves. And so I transformed our fireplace. My condominium is small; I see my fireplace from the kitchen counter, the archway to my writing space in the den, the windows on the porch, and the entrance hall. Each volume with its maroon cloth-bound cover and red leather label dominates my living space.

I first met David in 1978, not long after I'd divorced my second husband and my three grown sons, Charlie, Chris, and Michael, were attending colleges in the West. On a holiday in London I stayed at Brown's Hotel for a week of theater-going and it was that week when this tale began.

Polly's fireplace in Minneapolis

# Come for a Drink

## LONDON 1978

A few steps off the lobby of Brown's Hotel in Mayfair stood the phone booth, a polished dark oak cubicle with a glass door and walls covered in purple velour. Inside it smelled of stale tobacco and musky aftershave. I picked up the receiver and placed a twenty-pence coin into the slot atop the phone box. Was this the right time to call? Maybe I'd missed him. Had he already left for the office? It was early Monday morning, but as a rule Brits went in to work later than we did in Minneapolis.

Besides, David was expecting my call. Several days earlier when I checked into the hotel I had picked up his note. We had not met, but Newt Weed, a mutual friend and business colleague from Marsh McClennan, the New York-based insurance company, thought as we both enjoyed sailing we would enjoy each other's company. David was English, lived in London, and had built up Marsh's U.K./European network. In advance of my visit, Newt wrote to David. In response, David wrote a cordial note inviting me to phone him the moment I arrived in London.

But I didn't. Instead I arranged theater and dinner plans with some young friends from Minneapolis. This was my annual autumn holiday from my job at the Guthrie Theater, but I had reasons for not phoning besides all my theater tickets.

First I feared the unknown. What if he didn't like me? Perhaps worse, what if I didn't like him? I knew no Englishmen, and I wasn't looking for complications in my life. I was a fresh divorcee and needed some space before considering a new male relationship. So I waited until the next to last day of my visit to step into that phone booth. Inhaling the familiar scent, I listened to the phone ring several times.

He answered, and when I introduced myself, his first words were, "Hello, I was wondering when you would call." His voice sounded pleasantly British, a full tenor tone. And he didn't sound angry, just breezy. I tried to steady my voice.

"Well, yes, I'm sorry, I couldn't really call until now." The phone booth began to feel stifling hot. My palms sweated as I clung to the receiver.

"I would like to meet you," David said casually. "How about Wednesday night, come for a drink at my flat?"

"Yes, that would be just fine. I could do that," I said. I felt my scalp prickle. The air was oppressive, the scent acrid. I wanted to hold my breath. What was I saying? I was due to fly back to Minneapolis on Wednesday, due the next day to report for work.

"Could you have dinner?" David asked. His voice was interesting, persuasive.

"No, sorry, I can't. I have a ticket to *King Lear* at the Old Vic." How had I come up with that bold-faced lie? True, *King Lear* was playing at the Old Vic, and I had wanted to see it; Don Schoenbaum, Guthrie's Managing Director, was interested in hiring one of the actors. But I had no ticket and no idea what had propelled me to accept this date and to invent an evening at the Old Vic.

David's voice didn't waver. "All right," he said, "then come to my flat at 234 Cranmer Court, just off Sloane Avenue, at six o'clock and we'll have a drink before the play. It's a large block of red brick flats and I'm at the west end. You'll see the numbers on the doors."

"Thanks, I'll be there," I said. I cracked the door of the

phone booth so I could breathe. Next time I would call from my room.

"Looking forward to it. Ole Newt is a character," David chuckled.

"That's for sure," I said, "See you tomorrow." I hung up, but for a few minutes I stood still, remembering the warmth and humor of his voice.

Next I quickly called my boss to tell him I had secured a ticket for King Lear and would be returning home one day late. Then I called the Old Vic to reserve a seat.

In my room again, I pondered my decision. I was taking a chance, but what could possibly happen between us over a drink? Nothing, I assured myself, only an opportunity to hear that voice again, to meet a friend of friends. And for the next twenty-four hours I busied myself with favorite holiday activities, a walk in Green Park, a stop at an art gallery, a museum, a browse through a bookstore, lunch at a cafe on Piccadilly, and a play before a late dinner.

On Wednesday evening I boarded the Piccadilly Line and traveled underground to the South Kensington station. It was dark, warm and muggy for late October. I turned towards Sloane Avenue and walked several blocks south to Cranmer Court where I easily found his doorway. David answered my ring and buzzed me in.

As I rode the lift to the fourth floor I felt calm, and when the doors creaked open and I saw him standing at the elevator door, a handsome man, medium height, large-chested, with sandy hair and a wide smile, my body relaxed completely. He wore dark blue suit trousers, a blue striped shirt, the sleeves rolled up to the elbows, and no tie. I liked him at once.

I followed him into his flat, into the living room where a younger man hovered over sailing charts that lay on a large square coffee table.

"Richard Ford, Polly Brown, a friend of friends from Minneapolis. Richard and I are just going over some charts for his cruise to Normandy next summer." David gestured with his arm toward the maps.

Richard stood and offered a hand. "David taught me to sail and now he's helping me navigate," he said. Their camaraderie was evident, and the room felt instantly comfortable.

"What can I get you to drink?" David asked. "How about a dry martini? Americans love those—almost straight gin." He laughed, tossing his head. I knew he didn't expect me to ask for a martini.

"Oh no, I can't handle those. White wine would be perfect."

David stepped to a side table where a tray held large glass decanters of scotch and gin, bottles of red and white wine and a variety of glasses. I took mine and stood for a moment, taking some quiet breaths. I wasn't nervous, but I was pleasantly excited. I sat on a couch and sipped my wine as the two men went on studying maps and charts.

Obviously this meeting with Richard was important, yet David had managed to work me into his evening plans. The thought pleased me, and warmed by the flattery, I looked around the room. Paintings and prints covered white walls, mostly marine compositions and some fine small oil portraits of venerable Edwardian gentlemen and a few fresh Impressionist gouaches. I could see David had a keen eye. Two differently patterned chintz-covered couches surrounded the center table, now strewn with maps, and above the fireplace stood small metal figurines. In a corner by the windows a round table, with a patterned cotton cloth, held family photographs and delicate ivory and glass figurines. Along the wall on the desk top stood still more objets d'art.

This room had a lot to look at. But what I noticed most was that it felt happy and so, clearly, did David. I knew in that moment that I could spend more time in this place, with this person.

After a few more minutes the men finished their discussion of the Normandy harbors, Richard thanked David, shook my hand, and said his farewells.

Alone, David and I sat down to talk.

Conversation came easily. We spoke of our longtime friendship with the Weeds, about London and my love of theater, and we told each other about our grown children, my three sons and his three daughters. I even managed to admit to my two divorces, and then suddenly, all too soon, an hour had passed in what seemed only minutes, and it was time for me to leave. As I stood up I noticed six or seven large bound books stacked on a table behind me.

"What are these?" I asked.

"My scrapbooks—been keeping them since the war," David said. "Here's the one I'm working on now." He picked up the top book, placed it on the center table, and opened it at random. "Here's a good page. A photo of my granddaughter, Laura, with her pony and next to it a cutting of the winner of this year's Grand National race, and under those a photo of the four bronze horses from San Marco Square in Venice."

"Fascinating," I said, because the book was—far more interesting than ordinary scrapbooks stuffed with photos of trips.

David smiled. "This is scrapbooking, fitting the pieces together," he said as he closed the book.

I began to regret my theater ticket as David helped me with my coat, assuring me I'd have no trouble finding a taxi on Sloane Avenue. "Perhaps we'll see each other again, maybe next year or in Minneapolis. I come often to the States," he added, and then we said goodbye.

That night happened almost thirty years ago, and I recall nothing of the production of *King Lear*, a play that I must have seen at least five times. What I do remember is that after the performance, at 11 P.M., I exited a side door of the Old Vic into a rolling London fog and turned in the wrong direction. Finding no recognizable landmarks there, south of the Thames, I was soon lost, and then I heard heavy footsteps approaching and a harsh voice.

"Scared, little lady?"

I said nothing but began to walk as fast as I could, and to my relief soon overtook two tiny old ladies speaking in cockney accents. I called out "Hello, hello," and joined them explaining I'd become lost and had to find the closest underground. They took both my hands and said, almost in unison, "Oh, darlin', stay with us. Our bus will be coming soon."

And so we three traveled together on the bus about half a mile to the Elephant and Castle tube station where I boarded the train for Piccadilly Circus and walked safely the few blocks to my hotel. There I headed for a soft armchair in the Lounge and ordered a glass of white wine and a chicken sandwich. I was suddenly famished. I sipped and nibbled and reviewed my evening's adventures—out of the fog and into the light. That's what it felt like.

I closed my eyes, recalling David's brightly lighted flat, his lightly tanned face opening into a wide smile, his contagious laugh as he tipped his head. I remembered his rolled up shirt sleeves, his low, yet light voice, his clipped wit, his expressions, "Too clever by half," he had said when describing a current member of Parliament under scrutiny for some potentially disturbing scandal.

David was perceptive, frank, down to earth, his body and spirit reflecting his love of sailing, a basic and humbling skill. And when I described my Guthrie theater job and my election to the Board of Directors of the St. Paul Companies, he had said, "Well done, you, I must take you to Lloyds on your next visit." And when I had thanked him but mentioned that last year the St. Paul reinsurance people in London had entertained me and added we'd had very good champagne at lunch, he'd laughed and said, "We spare nothing for distinguished American guests."

I'd forgotten the play already, but I remembered every word he said.

Out of the fog, into the light.

After that night, I always took care whenever leaving a theater, especially in London where I was usually alone. And that night I chewed the last bite of the sandwich, small pieces of white meat, lettuce and lots of yellow mayonnaise on white bread, cut into small quarters with the crusts removed, and I knew in my bones I'd traveled out of the fog into the warmth.

It was twelve months later, during my October London visit, when David and I saw each other again. He arranged a theater performance and afterwards dinner at a restaurant near Brown's Hotel. At dinner, after we dissected the play, the production and the actors, he continued to ask questions about my job and life in Minneapolis. Then, suddenly, he wasn't paying attention to my responses, wasn't asking follow-up questions, and for the first time since we'd met, our conversation began to feel flat. When he paid the check and escorted me from the restaurant, I felt relief and disappointment. David Grose, I concluded, no doubt was seeing other women who were more interesting, more cosmopolitan than I was. I was just a Midwestern divorcee. He hailed a taxi and took my hand to help me into the cab. I turned to say goodbye, determined to remain cordial, thought I felt let down, hurt, and frustrated with myself. I had expected his full attention—not what now seemed a perfunctory obligation to entertain an acquaintance. The spark disappeared, but never mind, I told myself. After all, back home I had a great job and three marvelous sons who were finishing college and launching their own careers. I couldn't wallow in self-doubt. My boss expected me at the office in two days.

On the long flight home I read *Portrait of a Marriage*, Nigel Nicolson's story of his parents, Vita Sackville West and Harold Nicolson, and I decided that in the future, on my annual London forays, I wouldn't contact David. I would douse romantic expectations, refocus on family and work. Anyway a transatlantic romance was impractical, too time-consuming, with no future. That was the conscious conversation I had with myself, and yet, all the while I was remembering our light banter, our shared ideas, the way we'd so naturally tossed back and forth our impressions of T.S. Eliot's *Family Reunion*, the play we'd seen, the punch and energy that had fueled us for those first few hours.

Still, that was it for David Grose—a few unique London evenings and glimpses of a London life. Fleeting. That's how the story would end, and indeed four years passed before David and I again saw each other. It was the spring of 1983, after a long Minnesota winter, and Joan and Newt Weed told me David was traveling on business in the States. He would, they said, be visiting their house for the weekend; they invited me to their welcome party.

As I dressed for the evening, I wondered: Am I looking forward to seeing him after all this time? I wasn't entirely certain, though I had purchased a new dress for the occasion, a black and white print with red poppies scattered over the fabric. The weather had turned unseasonably warm for late April in Minnesota, and I wore no jacket. I parked my car at the bottom of the Weeds' driveway and there I felt a momentary chill, felt my stomach flutter and bounce. I knew I looked smart, and I felt pleased, eager, and anxious all at once. I smelled the air blowing on a soft wind across Lake Minnetonka, freshly free of ice. I looked down at the crocuses pushing their way up through tiny shoots of new grass.

I walked slowly up the driveway and trotted up the stairs to the front door. Then, at the top, I was suddenly looking right into David's eyes. He took a few steps forward and clapped his hands hard on my shoulders. His fingers pressed my shoulder blades.

"Well, here you are again, I suppose you've gotten married by now?" He smiled into my eyes.

"Are you kidding?" I said, "I won't ever get married again." I thought I was telling the truth.

"Ah, ha," he said, and he took my arm and walked me inside. "When did I last see you?" he asked.

"It'll be four years in October—when I was in London," I answered quickly.

"What have you been up to?"

"I'm now working for Hill and Knowlton and I hate my boss." Once again I felt completely easy with him. I was about to leave the company to take a development position with the University of Minnesota, and despite the interesting projects I'd worked on over the year, it was time for me to leave. I felt no compunction about sharing my news with David.

"You women. Maybe you should all stay at home."

I might have punched anyone else who made such a comment, but I knew he was joking. His eyes were laughing. I felt as if we'd had a continuing conversation all those years.

One of the guests approached. "Oh, David, so good to see you. Still sailing?" he asked and off David went, clasping hands, throwing his head back with laughter. He knew most of the people at the party from prior visits to Minneapolis and from a few sailing cruises in Florida, and with his ease he put everyone else at ease. I was aware of him as I moved around the party chatting with friends about the good weather and upcoming social events, and then he was at my side again.

"Why haven't we seen each other since '79?" he asked.

I couldn't be less than straightforward with this man—and so I told him that he'd seemed preoccupied that last evening, that I thought our time together had been less than inspired.

"What do you mean?" he asked as he moved closer.

"Well, you asked me this and that about work, but I didn't feel you really cared. And then you said we had to go—you were going to Brussels the next day." As I recalled the evening to him, I remembered more and more of the conversation, and though I didn't want to offend him, I had to be honest. If I couldn't do that, I would be betraying myself. I had learned through all the heartache of divorce that honesty and clarity were all that mattered, finally.

He looked directly at me. "Whenever it's time to cut off the evening, I always say I'm going to Brussels the next day. Keeps everyone guessing." He smiled, a broad grin and the skin around his eyes crinkled.

I was relieved my honesty hadn't offended him, and then Joan called us to the buffet supper, and once more David placed a huge hand on my shoulder and asked me to sit with him.

Sitting around the coffee table in the living room, eating our supper together, I began to feel lighthearted, flirty and lively, and before the evening was over, David asked me to join the Weeds and him the next day when they would move the motorboat from its winter shelter across the main bay of Lake Minnetonka to their summer dock. I had made other plans for Saturday but just as I had four-and-a-half years earlier, I scuttled those to spend time with David. This time I laughed to myself how easily I altered course.

Saturday dawned warm and sunny, and on the ride back to the dock, David and I sat on the stern seat, side by side, our khaki-trousered legs stretched out before us and lightly touching. I can still feel the current that rushed through me that day, a compelling force. Was that why Newt popped up with his camera, capturing us as we looked at each other? Again that strong hand and arm stretched around my shoulder. I snuggled under it. All these years later the photo rests in a silver frame on my bureau, and every time I look at it, I feel the warmth of the sun on my face, and the warmth of the man I was soon to love and marry.

David and Polly, Lake Minnetonka, April, 1983

# Cornish Hands

Following David's return to London at the end of April we talked frequently on the phone. He usually called me from his flat as he was preparing to go to work, so it was 2 A.M. Minnesota time when the phone woke me. I remember smiling and giggling when I heard his voice, and roused myself from a sound sleep. We discussed our next meeting, London in early June.

After a night at Brown's Hotel I was rested and ready for David when he appeared in the hotel lobby to escort me to his flat for this holiday. I looked up at him as he took my arm. I liked his smart blue suit, pink striped shirt, and blue tie, a man of bright colors. David opened the door of his BMW coupe, and smiled broadly as he helped me into my seat.

London was in full bloom. As we drove around Piccadilly Circus, down Haymarket to the Mall and Buckingham Palace, I breathed in the lush fragrance of the St. James' and Green Parks. Shrubs and borders of summer flowers—lilies, roses, and daisies—lined the paths that crisscrossed wide expanses of lawn. David pointed out the Palace Mews and the clock at Victoria Station as we continued down Eaton Place to Sloane Square and soon reached his new flat at 44 Elystan Place, across the street from Cranmer Court where we had met five years earlier. He had confessed to me that several years ago he had moved to a smaller flat when business friends overused the privilege of his extra bedroom.

Chelsea Green

The flat was on the top floor of a two-story building, five flats to each floor. I followed him up the stairs to an outside gallery where his door opened to a cubicle-sized foyer and four doors leading to four tiny rooms—the living room, its bow (bay) window overhanging the street, the bedroom, kitchen, and bath.

In the living room, or, as the English call it, sitting room, David had arranged the furniture as in his other flat, the sofas now snug against the square center table pushed to the west wall. Under the bow window a long marble-topped table held a stereo-radio combination; books were stacked on several other smaller tables, and lamps lit the paintings that covered every inch of wall space. He led me into the bedroom with its double bed, a desk and two tall French bureaus.

"Would you like to unpack?" He pointed to several empty bureau drawers. "I've made some space there and you can hang your dresses in the hall closet." As I began moving my clothes into place, we bumped into each other. But I didn't mind his tiny bachelor flat. It felt cozy.

Then I saw him frown as he studied my dresses. "Is that what you brought?" he asked, eyeing the red cotton summery dress, one of my favorites. "The women will be in black."

"But it's summer," I said, dismayed by his show of disappointment.

"Doesn't matter," he said firmly. "In London, black's the fashion."

"Oh, dear, I'll look so suburban." My heart contracted as I realized I was off to a poor start, but he smiled and said reassuringly, "Don't worry, you'll be all right."

We were to attend two cocktail parties that very night, he explained, and what I'd brought along would do.

It would have to. As a working woman, I wore suits and blouses. My few summer dresses, appropriate for Minnesota patio parties, were not designed for international capital city society, and later that evening, as I left the flat dressed in my red cotton, I felt like Dorothy from Kansas, setting out, naive and unprepared, on the Yellow Brick Road.

As we were driving to the party David offered instructions. "Avoid walking around the room saying, 'Hello, I'm Polly Brown.'" No one in London cared for those sorts of details, he explained, and as we made our way down the Royal Hospital Road to Cheyne Walk, my apprehension grew. Dorothy, alone and without guides, that was me.

We arrived at Johnny Churchill's house, and David swept us inside, introducing me to a few people clustered near the door. Then, by himself, he headed for a group across the room. I smiled sweetly as I turned to a silver-haired, blue-suited man and asked something like, "What was the most exciting thing you did today?" But by the time we'd been at Johnny's place for an hour, I felt I'd learned how to behave, though that was the same night I asked a partygoer where he liked to travel, only to learn he was the Swiss Ambassador to the United Kingdom. I listened to conversations about the approaching general election and the certain victory for Margaret Thatcher and the Tories, and I began to understand. This wasn't the warm, fuzzy

Midwestern nest where I had lived all my life, where I was a leader. Here I was an unknown, only David Grose's American girlfriend, his *new* girlfriend.

I knew little about David's past. I did know that he and his wife had divorced six years earlier, that their three daughters were grown, and two were married with children. They all lived in London. And I knew David had had, or maybe still did have, London girlfriends. I cautioned myself to play it cool, not to prickle or agitate over small problems. To succeed in London society, I would have to bide my time, be quiet, listen, develop well-placed conversation, discover when to enter a conversation with a witty or relevant point. I hoped, most of all, to put my country's best foot forward. And though I did feel cautious, I wasn't afraid.

I had a good job and education and I felt excited and confident I would measure up to David's standards and to those of his world. Even Londoners recognized the place I had attended college—familiar territory, New England, Smith College. But they knew little about the Midwest; my real home was a foreign place to most of them. I imagined they thought we lived on icy terrain, in tepees or igloos, and I meant to unravel at least some of those misconceptions.

Back at the flat later that first evening, David and I sat around the center table talking about our plans for the next few days. He opened his large black leather engagement diary, and watching him with studied care, I noticed I think for the first time his hands.

"Your hands are square," I said.

He smiled. "These are Cornish hands, my heritage, hands of the working people. My people worked in the tin mines. A great-uncle was a well-known mining engineer."

I studied them—square and large, with well-clipped nails and light tufts of hair.

He leaned forward as he went on, proud to trace his family history. "The Groses come from Penzance, Cornwall. My grandmother was proud of her heritage. She always stated she wasn't

English, she was Cornish, and crossing the Tamor river was entering a foreign country."

Something inside me relaxed then. I was gaining ground with David; he was sharing personal stories, and by the time I fell asleep that night, I felt closer to this man with his square hands and mysteriously hooded eyes than I had with anyone in many years. As we embraced I nuzzled into his chest and inhaled a herby, basil smell, distinctively his. It was lovely, a scent I would forever after recall.

Each weekday morning about 9 A.M. David left the flat to go to his office. He walked smartly across the street to his BMW, opened the door, sat down, started the engine, rotated back the roof cover, and pushed his hand up to wave to me. I was at the bedroom window dressed in a bright red, Tahitian-print dressing gown, waving happily at this man I was growing to love, and this small sequence became a morning ritual. Even now, each time I open my closet and see the gown, I remember those moments, the spontaneous joy in our waves.

And every morning after David's car pulled away, I bathed, dressed, and set off to do errands: grocery store, cleaners, and flower stall for David's favorites—lilies, from the green grocer. Just to the right of the downstairs door of our flat was the Chelsea Green, a small triangular space with two large cherry trees surrounded by small shops and stalls. Early in my visit, David introduced me to the owners, Paul the greengrocer, Paul the chemist, John the ironmonger, Bill the fishmonger, whose scratchy voice after several bouts of throat cancer was almost inaudible. And there was Rose, the tiny laundress, with jet-black dyed and permed hair, who ruled the roost. Since David's flat was too small for a washing machine, he took weekly bags of wash to Rose, and they had become friends.

The neighborhood boasted several delicatessens. I especially liked the Italian one where all the servers wore straw boater hats. On subsequent visits to London, when my flights arrived on weekday mornings, I would pick up David's flat keys from one

Polly at David's flat; London, June, 1983

of the Italians, and I enjoyed his conspiratorial wink as he offered me the bunch of keys.

On that first visit, and on every other visit after that, I couldn't resist buying flowers. Everywhere I looked there were flower stalls—next to the underground stations, beside the green grocers, along the Kings Road. Like Virginia Woolf's Clarissa Dalloway I set off each morning in search of a new bouquet. Flowers grew in abundance all year long in this temperate climate, and as a girl accustomed to long winters without such blooms, I was in heaven. I couldn't resist buying bunches, baskets, and bouquets of lilies, daffodils, tulips, irises, roses, and all the other perennials whose complicated names I could never remember but whose fragrances, shapes, and colors I adored.

Each day I investigated a series of new side streets and came to know the broad neighborhood, bounded on the east by Buckingham Palace and Green Park, the north by Hyde Park, the south by the Thames and Battersea Park, and the west by Gloucester Road. As on that first visit, I never tired of London's sounds—the taxi klaxon, the double-decker buses' snort as they pulled into and away from the curb. I was forever intoxicated by the smells of the city—the many varieties of ethnic food wafting from the food shops and cafes. And I delighted to hear the voices of the people— different accents, exotic dress, dozens of languages.

I was falling in love with the city, as well as with David.

Our favorite restaurant was Au Bon Accueil, a cozy bistro where the neighbors frequently gathered for French country cooking. And even while I had no idea that this charming neighborhood and marvelous set of characters, this whole glorious city, would eventually become my home, I did try hard that first visit to acclimate, to explore and to understand and to respect David's world. One day he asked me to buy him some special buttons, Navy uniform buttons, for the jacket he wore to his prestigious yacht club, the Royal Yacht Squadron, but he explained that only one tailor on Savile Row stocked these. I found the place, bought the buttons, and as I sat in the flat sewing them on, I felt important. I took care to pay attention to detail, making sure the anchor on the button stood straight up, and that evening when I handed him the jacket, he grinned. "Well done, you," and I beamed. That was high praise.

"Next time you're here we'll sail across the Solent to Cowes and have lunch at the Squadron," he said, and warmth flooded my body. Next time. I wondered when that next time would be, but before I could wonder for long, David began to speak of another trip. Soon. We laughed when I reminded him of a fortuitous coincidence—the Humphrey Institute at the University of Minnesota had a reciprocal program for postgraduate students from the U.K. to study at the Institute. I would build and expand this enterprise.

One night on this first visit David and I attended a chamber music concert at St. John's Church in Smith Square near Parliament. Two of David's close friends joined us, and afterwards we had dinner at the Thorold's house in Notting Hill. I learned that they and David alternated each month selecting a concert at a baroque concert hall or church venue and hosting the dinner afterwards, and though I did not know it that night, we would, for years, continue the tradition.

As the weekend of that first visit approached, David spoke about plans to sail on the Solent, and I began to worry about my sailing prowess. I had sailed on ocean waters, knew about tides and tying the proper knots, but I harbored a long-held anxiety.

Growing up on Lake Minnetonka, I thought sailing should have come naturally, but even on a sunny day with a light breeze, I never felt secure in flat-bottomed scows. As a light and quick-moving person I crewed for some of the boys I knew, providing ballast on their D or E boats during a hotly contested racing season. I would dart from one side to the other to create the proper angle of the boat to the wind, and I loved moving quickly, ducking under the boom to reach the windward position and hanging my bottom over the side to stabilize the angle.

But in a flash, a cold front moving swiftly across Minnesota could appear to produce relentless squalls, building to huge proportions. Capsizing terrified me. I was never a strong swimmer. My merely adequate crawl could never survive a calamitous ocean sea; I felt severely tested in our shallow lake when sudden squalls hit and the fleet of D and E boats turned over like dominoes. Thrown overboard, I usually wound up under the boat, snarled in lines and as I came to the surface dodging floorboards sprung loose from the boat's floor. Waves built up, temperatures plummeted as the front passed through. We crew members struggled to right the scow and climbed aboard, shivering. When the officials called the race because of fears of worse weather, parents patrolling in their small motorboats would often toss us a line and tow us to the Yacht Club—to safety and mugs of hot cocoa.

Not until my second marriage to Ted Brown did I let go of these memories and fears. Ted was an excellent sailor with experience in ocean sailing. Over the Easter holiday break we gathered our respective children—my boys, Charlie, then 12, Chris, 11, and Michael, 8, along with Ted's older ones—for a cruise on the Gulf Coast, from Tampa Bay to Boca Grande. I listened to Ted explain that these these boats with their heavy centerboards could not tip over or capsize, and so I began to feel safe, relieved that I would not inflict my own fears on my children. Still, when I glimpsed a thin line of a front on the horizon, my body stiffened.

I did, though, enjoy Ted's boat as a holiday home. I liked providing a comfortable nest for my brood, provisioning at each port, standing in the galley cooking simple pastas and scrambled eggs. I liked the discipline of conserving water and acknowledging limited space, the early morning rising and turning in at night snug in a sleeping bag or under a duvet. Sometimes I slept on deck amidst some of the children, counting the stars and watching the moon rise up on the horizon. And so all that week as David spoke of sailing on the Solent, I held that calming memory close, so that by Saturday morning I felt ready to be David's crew.

We drove to the Beaulieu river to sail on *Sall*, his wooden fishing smack. The boat was moored up the river from the Gins Farm Yacht Club, a part of the Royal Southampton Club. This, David told me, was a weekend pattern that he'd kept for many years, a welcome release from London's hectic social and business pace. The Yacht Club bosun took us in his dinghy to *Sall*, and we raised the mainsail and motored away from the buoy, heading down river.

Once in the Solent waters, David cut the motor, and we were under sail, and as I inhaled the salty air, I felt alive and free. Several races were in progress, and I watched in admiration as David skillfully maneuvered *Sall* through the fleet. We tacked west along the shore of the Isle of Wight to Yarmouth, entered the harbor, and there found a berth at the marina. That night we ate supper at the George Hotel, and overlooking the water and the lights of harbor entrance, David began to tell me all about his love for the sea. As a teenager, he said, he had canoed alone down the Thames River from Oxfordshire to London, camping each night by a friendly pub located near a lock. When he talked about his adventures on the water, his eyes glistened.

He had grown up in North London; his father had built office buildings in the U.K. and Canada. David's mother was born in Toronto. I asked a few questions and discovered that his memories about his childhood were vague, but it wasn't until a year later when I met Molly, his younger sister and only sibling, that I learned he simply didn't care enough to recall details. Molly filled in the blanks I sought, but I never probed. I respected David's privacy. I understood that as a young man he had set his sights high, looking to a future beyond North London. His parents had sent him to a boarding school, part of the London Guild system, that I knew, but his most vivid memory of that school was learning to appreciate classical music; the house master in the adjacent room played Bach, Mozart, and Handel on his gramophone.

When he was 19, in 1939, David joined the navy, and it was the memory of those war years that stuck. Starting with his service on the lower deck of the *Berwick* and a tour of duty on the Russian Convoys on the North Sea, he became a maritime person, and that persona never left him.

"I am often reminded of those days, 1941," David continued, "the Navy and the lower deck of the *Berwick* where we stretched out our hammocks each night."

The H.M.S. *Berwick* was part of a fleet of Allied ships called the Russian Convoy, protecting the Allied supply boats from German torpedoes as they made their way with supplies and materiel up the North sea, across the Norwegian and Barents Seas to Murmansk in Northern Russia. It was a dangerous mission; the convoy was a sitting duck for German submarines. Standing watch on the deck in temperatures way below zero, men's faces froze and the weight of the clothing made it impossible to move.

David told me of his respect for his fellow sailors and officers and for the discipline of the Navy that grew with each year of

David on *Sall*, Beaulieu River, U.K., June, 1983

his service. The men forged a special bond on a Navy vessel, serving for months and living in close quarters aboard a moving object vulnerable to attack at any time. After that tour of duty he applied to officer school and served in Greece, Gibraltar, and finally Rome, at the end of the war.

"The Navy made me," he said, and he told me that some of his fellow Naval officers introduced him to influential insurance men at Lloyd's of London, hence the beginning of his insurance career.

I suddenly looked around the dining room and noticed we were the only patrons remaining. I nodded at David who signaled the headwaiter who, with relief, quickly offered the check.

After dinner we walked around the harbor, past the Lifeboat station to our quay and *Sall*, and there we slipped into our sleeping bags on the side bunks of the cozy saloon and slept peacefully, lulled by the lapping water.

Sunday morning's church bells woke us early, and David prepared our breakfast: juice, coffee, and slices of thick bread held by a long fork over the gas flame to give each side a crisp black coating. With lots of butter and marmalade, the toast was perfect.

Soon we set sail down the Solent on the ebbing tide, heading home. That's when, suddenly, the sky darkened and rain began to fall. The temperature plummeted, and hail the size of golf balls spun from the heavens into *Sall's* cockpit. Quickly we pulled on ponchos, and I bailed out the hail as David guided us into the Beaulieu River.

And amazingly, there in the river was Richard Ford, whom I had met five years before in David's London flat. Richard, with a few friends, was sailing his boat back to his river buoy. We shouted to each other, lowered our sails, and moored close to each other on our respective buoys. Then we all climbed into the bosun's dinghy for the ride to the club.

Richard and I exchanged a peck on each cheek, the usual English greeting, and we walked from the pontoon to the clubhouse where we quickly found a table for drinks and a simple lunch. After that chaotic morning, fish and chips and frozen peas tasted like an extravagant feast.

I relaxed as I watched and listened to the easy camaraderie between these men of the sea. In them I saw vitality, respect for nature, for the changing weather, the swooping sea gulls and tiny shore birds, the soft damp air coursing down the river, the rhythms of the tides. I turned to look out the wide picture windows of the club at the boats tugging at their buoys all the way downriver to the tip of the its mouth, and like these men and this lively world, I felt filled and overflowing with life.

# Career Path

I'll take a few steps back to describe my passion for drama that led to my career path and to the moment when I would travel to London to be with David.

Over forty years ago Tyrone Guthrie brought his dream to Minnesota, America's heartland, far from Broadway's commercial pressures. He established a professional acting company to perform a season of four classical, or potentially classical, plays in repertory. One night an actor plays the title role in *Hamlet*, the next he's a waiter in *Private Lives*. The new Guthrie Theater opened on May 7th, 1963, to resounding success across the country and the English-speaking world. Within a few years it had evolved from a repertory summer stage to a year-round enterprise producing plays on its main stage and in a second experimental theater. The theater produced works by Shakespeare, Ibsen, Chekhov, and Americans Miller, Williams, O'Neill, as well as new work by up-and-coming playwrights.

I joined the Board of Directors of the Guthrie, drawn to professional theater from a childhood passion for a world of make-believe. In our backyard, under a willow tree's protective leafy skirt, I felt its magic, explored my dreams and invented stories. I carried these in my head to our living room, and there, behind a drapery drawn across the piano in the bay window, I prepared for my earliest performances. I stepped out in front of the family audience, dutifully gathered to see my dramatic routines, sweeps and bows. Dressed in chiffon, one of my mother's trousseau dresses, its hem trailing on the ground, I offered my earliest inventions, swooping to a finish to the light patter of family hands. Was it stepping forward to an audience, speaking the first words, sensing a glowing flush as I took a curtain call, turning from right to left, and acknowledging the accolades that drew me to the stage? I think partly it must have been an unquenchable thirst for approval, a magnetic cord, that pulled me the way it pulls so many of us.

After the Guthrie's 1963 opening, a group of us volunteers gave public tours throughout the building. Even there, with no performance in progress, I felt the magic, and when I was backstage during a performance in the dressing rooms replete with make-up lights and mirrors, greasepaint, talc and perfume, the heat and moisture, sweat and skin, I felt the heat of theater. "Darling," came the age-old chorus, "you were wonderful, absolutely marvelous." To touch the actors' trembling hearts. No one ever asked, "How was I?" That question was simply implied.

And nine years later I was elected chairman of the theater's Board of Directors. I was proud and pleased to lead the board, but as the months went by I knew deep down I craved a full-time job, a salary, and professional accountability. Two factors drove my ambition; the first, I realized that in order to divorce my second husband I would need an income of my own, and two, that I had a dream to use my education and energy to forge a real career, to push beyond the traditional boundaries of women of my age and social standing, and test myself in the professional, salaried work world. Over thirty years ago, this movement from volunteer to paid worker was new. I knew how to fund-raise and I knew how to lead an organization. I wanted to compete in the business world, to stretch upwards to the Glass Ceiling.

And at this time the theater was realigning its administrative staff to add a development director position. After discussions with several friends, mentors in the workplace, and Don Schoenbaum, Guthrie's Managing Director, in July 1974 I became the Development Director, using my volunteer-honed skills to become an executive in nonprofit administration

On the following day at 7:30 A.M. I took possession of my first job and office, a small cubicle fitted with desk, typewriter, files, in-and-out trays, and bookcases, and an open door to all the staff with whom I had worked on so many projects. I was thrilled to be among them as a peer. I would never look back.

With gusto, I plunged into my job. On the home front, my teenage sons were proud of me and thrilled I wasn't home to remind them not to be late for their summer jobs or to pick up their rooms. Everyone was a winner!

From the first work day at the Guthrie Theater, I understood I had much to learn from the theater's administrative executives, Don Schoenbaum and Don Michaelis. They taught me about accountability, taking on tasks and being responsible for their success, or failure. Don Michaelis used an expression called "throughput." At the end of the day, he explained, I should empty my inbox, complete the tasks, and sweep clean my desktop. The notion still makes sense to me.

Don Schoenbaum was a most respected union negotiator, meeting and favorably determining theater-related contracts with myriad unions. He could stare down the toughest union representatives. He never blinked first. From him I learned about "sticking to my guns," not wavering, but planning a position or a strategy, testing, and executing it.

The Guthrie was a lively place, collegial, affirming, thoughtful, and trusting. Each day was new and exciting. Surrounded by actors, technicians, set builders, sound technicians, and a skilled administrative staff, I reveled. Arriving early was key, time to organize my day, then review with my staff plans and actions to solicit contributions from a growing number of local and national corporations, and from community individuals and private foundations.

Our team worked closely with the marketing department, planning events for corporate and important individuals from the public and private sectors of the Twin Cities and the Midwest region. We coordinated efforts with the education and touring department to develop corporate and individual support from communities around the region. We understood that the Guthrie enriched communities, attracted employees and families, and increased the economic strength of that area. An education component accompanied each touring production to work within the local school systems. That was the way to build future audiences.

To cultivate financial support from the major corporations within the metro area, my colleagues and I organized informal lunches at the theater for the community's corporate leaders. At these lunches Guthrie program department heads presented information about their work and emphasized the theater's cultural and economic value to the community and region. After one of these events in early 1976, Ron Hubbs, chairman of the St. Paul Companies, one of the country's largest property and casualty insurance companies, phoned to ask me to join the company's board of directors.

I was flattered and surprised, and I wondered what could I bring to this board. Ron assured me that as the first woman director of a company with 60 percent female employees, I'd bring a sorely needed woman's point of view to the board's policy-making. He went on to talk of my administrative experience and community longevity. In those days that was sufficient criteria for this position.

Again I consulted with mentors, and Don Schoenbaum encouraged me to accept the directorship. He said it was an honor for the Guthrie to have a staff member serve on the board of a large publicly held corporation.

So, proud and humble at the same time, I accepted. Around the board room table sat some of the most competent and farsighted business and professional men in the community, and from those men I learned not only about the property and casualty insurance business but about corporate collegiality, give-and-take at this level of deliberation. At the meetings I listened carefully before offering an opinion or idea. And my fellow directors seemed to welcome my contributions. One of the directors, Rob Ridder, and I lunched together from time to time to discuss new company strategies and an effective role for outside directors. I valued these meetings and his helpful advice, and I set out to find a unique way to further my board contributions.

I took a special interest in the women employees, interviewing and discussing issues with many women from a variety of departments. I listened closely to their desire for flexible time, such as time off to take a child with a chronic disease to a doctor without losing status or a promotion. I brought their concerns to the board. My work credo was simple: each woman should have an opportunity to reach her potential for an executive or professional position. I understood that my community background and the network I had offered me a head start, and I felt compelled to open as many doors as I could for the women working at the St. Paul Companies.

Our board meeting lunches were held in the executive dining room. We directors sat around a long mahogany table enjoying a three-course meal served by a uniformed staff. At the conclusion of my first board lunch, a waiter appeared with a box of cigars. He walked right past me.

"Pardon me," I said, tapping his arm. "I'll have one, thank you." He bowed and turned back to me, and I selected a fine Cuban cigar to bring back to one of my colleagues at the Guthrie. I refused to be set apart from the men, and I continued accepting a cigar whenever offered.

Often during informal committee meetings around a small table, a director would lean back in his chair and place his feet comfortably on the table. After one of these "old boy" gestures, I leaned back in my chair, tucked my suit skirt safely under me, and placed my feet in black leather pumps on the table. Laughter ensued, and a moment later all feet found the floor.

This board membership led to another. Within months, I was elected to the board of Tonka Corporation, the parent company of Tonka Toys. As Tonka was a smaller organization, we directors had more a direct view of the corporate operations. One of our first tasks was to fire the CEO and hire his replacement.

In 1977 the Board of Governors of the Minneapolis Club, a prominent downtown men's club, voted to accept women members before a change in the tax law forced them to act. The following year the Club elected me its first woman member. I was thrilled to be recognized.

The Minneapolis Club grill was a popular and a formidable den of men. They joined together at the "cheese table" or sat at small tables, hailing each other as the room filled. The room exuded male camaraderie, and I relished the opportunity to join my peers. On a midweek workday in early September 1978, I made my first reservation for me and Rob Ridder. Jerry, the maître d', placed us in an anteroom I called the Caboose, a tight overflow space opening off the main room, far from the hurly-burly of the grill. I looked around. I didn't like it one bit. One meal there was enough. If I was going to be a full-fledged member of this club, I would insist on my rightful place. So after that day I asked Jerry to give me a table in the grill, and he always reserved a prominent table in the middle of the room. "This all right for you, Mrs. Brown?" he asked, flashing his broad grin. Goodbye Caboose, I said to myself as I ordered a chicken salad and looked skyward at the Glass Ceiling.

By 1982 I had arrived at a career crossroads. I knew it was time for me to leave the Guthrie to explore new challenges within the public relations field, and time for the theater to hire someone with fresh ideas and skills. I began the process with a consulting job at Hill and Knowlton, a national public relations firm that had recently opened a Minneapolis office. Bill Wells, manager of the local office, asked me to help them develop contacts and work with nonprofit organizations. By then I'd worked enough with corporate heads to be able to read Bill's private agenda; he wanted my knowledge of the inner structure of the community and my help in capturing its key players.

Initially Bill and I worked smoothly together. He was courteous, respectful, and open to my ideas; he praised my work. Five months later, I asked Bill for a full-time position. Not overly enthusiastic, he agreed, but he added that I could not expect a salary comparable to the Guthrie. I would have to prove myself with the firm's corporate accounts. That was okay by me; I liked the energy and the expertise of the Hill and Knowlton marketing and financial relations executives and was eager to build new skills working with a variety of clients and projects. In June of 1982 I bade farewell to my beloved theater, and its secure and affirming work culture.

Bill and my new full-time colleagues greeted me warmly. Then Bill told me I would work long hours on difficult projects, and gave me my first task: to write a brief reply to a corporate client summarizing its pressing problem and providing an analysis and resolution of the issue, and return it to him within an hour. With my heart pounding, I fought to think fast and write cogently. He slashed black lines through much of the text. I soon learned that he would react consistently this way to my work. Any honeymoon was over. I couldn't understand why I didn't please him or why he rejected my work without constructive criticism. I agonized over every written assignment knowing it would return crisscrossed with black marks and deleted sentences. He forbade any rebuttal or discussion; just swallow and get on with it.

Then, I realized Bill was a liar. Often he dodged with false alibis important appointments with prospective or long-term corporate clients, and sent one of his staff as a substitute. Before long I knew his real motive in hiring me was to exploit my connections to community leaders. Ambitious and desperate for rewards from the Chicago regional office, he aggressively sought, through fair or foul means, contacts and new contracts. I often overhead him on the phone assuring his Chicago boss that, "Polly would deliver the goods"—confidential information about my corporate friends. And I refused to do so.

As time went on, I worked over weekends and longer hours each day. Many mornings I arrived at 4 A.M. to handle some emergency from an East Coast client. At lunchtime I ate snack foods at my desk purchased on a midmorning trawl through the Skyway convenience shops, and I took off time only to attend the St. Paul Companies and Tonka Corporation board and committee meetings. When I returned to the office, a scowling Bill would give me additional assignments guaranteed for late night completion. I just smiled to myself as I now understood his weakness; he was jealous.

Three days a week I left for night classes at Metropolitan State University. I took courses in marketing, financial public relations, accounting, and writing. I was so close to getting my B.A. degree that this final push made sense. Over thirty years earlier I had chosen marriage over a college degree, but I had never let go of a lifelong dream of a college degree, and night school offered the opportunity.

Things were tightening at the office. The straw that broke my back was a plane trip to Chicago to meet with Bill's boss and a top staff person of Sears, a corporate prospect. I shivered in Hill and Knowlton's suite at the top of a huge tall hotel as a cold January wind ripped against the plate glass windows. The dinner meeting was held in the suite. My role was to provide inside information, private stories that revealed any weaknesses of Sears' competitors in Minneapolis. I refused to sing against my friends. I sat in silence sipping my wine as they plied me with questions. Later as I tried to sleep against the noise of rattling windows, I wondered about the Ceiling. Surely one could touch and splinter the Ceiling without compromising one's integrity.

Fortunately, one of our pro bono clients, the Hubert Humphrey Institute of Public Affairs at the University of Minnesota, rescued me. Harlan Cleveland, Dean of the Institute, was looking for a development director. I saw my niche, and an honest mentor. I jumped at the chance. At the end of May I quit Hill and Knowlton, and in mid-June of 1983 I joined the Humphrey Institute, and at the same time received my B.A. from Metro State University.

Joyfully, each morning I leapt from bed eager for the work I loved, a job where I could concentrate on the issues within one organization instead of dividing the day between widely diverse corporate projects. An experienced diplomat, a former U.S. Ambassador to NATO, Harlan created a collegial atmosphere at the Institute. He spoke slowly and carefully to convey his broad intelligent thinking and fresh concepts of governance.

Before long, Geri Joseph. my good friend and a former U.S. Ambassador to the Netherlands, joined the team to work with Harlan on international program development. And I worked closely with all the department heads to define our fundraising priorities. But, as I was falling in love with a Brit, I was particularly interested in the Institute's U.K. program.

Within the U.K., prominent members of the Tory and Labour parties had raised funds to honor former U.S. Vice President Humphrey. They visualized opportunities for their young civil servants and politicians to work at the Institute for a period of several months or a year to learn about the American practice of public affairs. And Harlan saw a unique challenge for the Institute to make its mark in the U.K., where scholars, professional and business people had long favored the long-standing public affairs institutes at Harvard, Princeton, and Stanford. So he gave me permission to make several trips to London to meet with the U.K. Committee. At that time no one could measure the results of those trips.

# Tenerife: The Canary Islands, March 1984

The snow was blowing past my office window, a typical winter day in Minnesota, when David phoned from London. He suggested a winter holiday, a week on Tenerife, one of the Canary Islands off the coast of Spain. Some friends had given him their flat for the end of February, and I told him I would try to get away. I was spending more and more time on the Humphrey Institute's U.K. program and less time developing resources for the entire organization, which I believed had not distressed my colleagues so far.

I asked my boss for a ten-day leave of absence on the condition that I would work over the weekends for the next month to make up for lost time. I remember his exhausted smile as he gave permission.

"Any chance we can get this guy over here?" he asked.

"I don't think so," I said. "He's a real Brit," and although I had his okay for this trip, I knew he was measuring my travels. I could feel my luck running out. But I so wished to be with David that I took the risk.

Weeks later, only hours after I'd arrived in London, David and I flew to Tenerife on a night flight. I slept on his shoulder, and we landed in predawn darkness.

The guest flat was spacious and pleasantly furnished, overlooking Playa de las Americas and the public beach. The sand, charcoal gray, a mixture of crushed lava and sand imported from the Sahara desert, gave an eerie cast to the seascape and startled me at first glimpse. I had never traveled to these volcanic islands.

After shopping for groceries we settled into a delightful daily routine, breakfast in the flat and a walk to the harbor to check on fishing and other marine activity. Eager for the sun's rays after a long Minnesota winter, I stretched out on a cement quay while David strode around the fishing fleet and sailboats, talking to whomever he could find on a boat, or rather gesturing to them since he didn't speak Spanish.

Then in our rented car we drove around the island, circling the massive snowcapped Mt. Teide, the highest mountain in Spain. Banana plantations and groves of laurel trees covered the verdant north coast. Exotic bird-of-paradise plants dotted the landscape, in stark contrast to southern Tenerife with its rusty brown rocky peaks striped with shiny veins of lava flows. David sped around the winding mountainous roads, hugging gray rocky cliffs while I watched intently; the chain link fence didn't look strong enough to hold the car should it veer off into space. This was exciting stuff for a girl from the flat terrain of middle America, each moment increasingly exhilarated to be in love with with this vital man.

Each day we stopped in different villages and tiny harbors. We ate local fish stew and chunks of hot bread at simple, smoky cafes. David had a keen eye for the perfect photograph, a few of me draped over a railing or a wharf stone bollard, but mainly he focussed on the village people, the fishermen or the women selling their wares or a group of four men playing cards and smoking cigarettes outside a village bar in Los Cristianos. As their attention focused on the game, they didn't see David approach to take the shot, and his photo captured this intensity. To me this photo represented the camaraderie of the island people, and I placed a copy in my photo album.

Our evenings fell into a quiet pattern; we stayed in the flat with wine, tinned soup, and chocolate cookies, followed by David's vain attempts to teach me backgammon.

Toward the week's end, I began to feel sad about saying goodbye. I didn't want to let go. There seemed so much at stake. In truth I was scared, uncertain about our future. We had been crisscrossing the Atlantic every few months for almost a year, and my heart was leading me away from my homeland, but I wasn't sure how much longer we could bear the expense of these visits, and I knew I was walking a tightrope at work, one that was beginning to fray.

David and I had never talked about the future. I had no idea how he felt about a long-term relationship. "Marriage" was a word never spoken. I was well aware of the scars from his first marriage, his guilt and anger, some of which he'd shared with me, and I wanted more than anything to share joy, not conflict, or to endure any more pain.

I was completely in love with him, entranced and intrigued by his charm and affection, by his Englishness, his vigor and gentleness. At home in Minneapolis, I thought of him constantly, his face and voice coasting through my mind as I tried to concentrate on my work. Each day in Minnesota was one closer to the day I would see him again, and those days in between were feeling dull and heavy.

Often David told me he loved me. He whispered one night, "You have touched my heart," and yet I wondered. He was an enthusiastic flirt, and had enjoyed many girlfriends during and after his marriage. I knew he kept in touch with a few favorites.

And now, in Tenerife, I stood in the doorway of our bedroom watching him turn back the duvet on the bed. Time for lovemaking, and finally I said it.

"David, I want to come live with you." My words hit the air like bullets.

He looked up. "Shouldn't we think about this a bit?" He didn't move. But I had to go on, I couldn't waste this moment, we had so few left before I would fly home.

"I want to come to London to live with you." There, I had said it again.

He moved to me and said softly, "What about your job?"

"I can bring my U.K. work here and develop it, and give up the rest." What was I saying? Give up the rest. My life. The career I had worked for years to develop? I was at the top of my fundraising profession, and I was willing to throw it all away. Could I truly mean that? And leave my children? My parents? My secure Minneapolis nest?

"You'd be willing to give up your life in Minney? Your family?" His words brought back a flood of memories of homesick years I'd spent in boarding school and college. Was I crazy?

"Yes, I would. I'll go back from time to time. The children are grown now. They have babies of their own," I said. My words sounded like blocks of wood. What did they mean?

"Let's think about it for a while." David kissed me. My heart was a drum, beating hard. I felt like a peeled grape, not sure I would ever grow skin again. Why hadn't he wrapped me in his arms? Why hadn't he said, "Yes, yes, soon." Instead, he offered only a vague promise to talk later, maybe months later.

When David and I were together, our precious moments were filled with attention and love. Would they continue? Or had I just smashed our crystal bubble? Would I now become a seldom-seen girlfriend? Or would he walk away? I swallowed hard. I knew better than to pursue the subject. I had made my point. We both turned away to take off our clothes and climb into bed, and then, as if nothing monumental had been said, as if the evening had been about moving backgammon men around the board, David took me in his arms and touched me, moving slowly and gently. I responded, pleased that I had not upset our nightly lovemaking. Soon he was asleep, but I lay sleepless on my back, not moving. I could hear his measured breathing, regular in and out, sprinkled with occasional snorts, a punctuation mark, a man sleeping peacefully, undisturbed, certain that the moon was traveling across the southern sky, that dawn would break as the sun rose above the harbor, glinting off the spars of the sailing fleet. I watched a three-quarter moon shuttering through the puffs of cloud. I feared I would never sleep, but at long last I drifted off.

The next morning after breakfast we took a ferry to Gomera, a smaller, mountainous, lush island. Through cedar forests and stands of laurel trees wrapped in moss, orange groves, and potato farms, we bused to Alto de Garcijonay. At a general store we bought a picnic—salami, white cheese, bread, and a bottle of water—and found a small park nearby. Leaning on a large rock, we basked in the hot noon sun. I poured water into two cups.

David picked up the salami and cut two slices with a pocket knife. He closed the blade and flipped the knife into the air, catching it in his fist.

"Had this since the Navy. I remember buying it in Portsmouth before we sailed up the North Atlantic." He looked straight at me. "I think you forget how much older I am than you. Twelve years is a big difference." My heart sank. We had been over this subject before. I assured him our age difference didn't matter. It never had.

"Sure you wouldn't be happier with someone your own age, someone from Minney?" Oh, this was sounding better, I thought, drinking in the sun and the warmth of his love.

"Now, back to your bombshell last night," he continued. "What about your life? Could you leave it? Tell me."

"Yes," I said. I was certain I could leave. I couldn't say another word.

"You wouldn't be homesick?" I shook my head. I was willing to risk it. Why did he ask me that?

And then he reached out to me. "I want you to come very much, maybe later this year."

I fell into him, sending the water cups tumbling. Here at last was his answer. After six years alone, I would again have a partner, and it was then I think I realized how deep down I yearned for a true love, for the security that I'd never had.

"Hey, hey, look, there goes our water." David laughed, pulling back. "Don't you want that piece of salami?" He nibbled a piece. He liked his food.

But now floodgates open, my appetite felt reserved for him, for us. "When should I plan to come? Maybe November after the election?" Minnesota's Walter Mondale, our former Vice President and a Minneapolis acquaintance, was challenging Ronald Reagan. But I needed David to confirm a date. By November I could be ready to move.

"That sounds good, I'll fix up a few things in the flat," David smiled, "like maybe another closet." I wondered where he would find room for a new closet. Furniture and paintings covered every inch of the wall space, and he hung his blue suits—always blue, not gray or brown, but dark blue—in a tiny closet in the sitting room. In order to pick out the right suit, he used a flashlight to distinguish their textures. I had been using a minute foyer closet above the Hoover for my clothes. David told me the new closet would fit in the bedroom behind the bed which stood out from the wall, and I laughed, agreeing it was a perfect place. Now he had truly confirmed my move.

That evening we found a cozy restaurant to celebrate our plans. The next night we flew back to London, arriving in time for me to catch a morning connecting flight to Minneapolis. I was tired but now I knew his love was real, and with his commitment I felt joyful, without anxiety. I was going home to organize the move, poised for the most adventurous path I'd ever taken.

On the long flight home I closed my eyes and my thoughts rambled over familiar terrain. Is risk a part of every change? It seemed I had always put myself on the firing line, rushing pell mell into situations without analyzing the potential fallout. All those years ago, in 1952, when I accepted my first husband's proposal over the telephone. "Of course, I'll marry you in three weeks." Eben Dobson was a handsome Air Force second lieutenant, jet pilot, Minneapolis native, and family friend then training for an overseas tour in Korea. We'd dated only briefly between his training programs, when one November evening he had phoned me from Fort Worth to ask me to marry him.

And years later, married to Ted Brown, I'd left housewifely security to seek a job. From the Guthrie position, I was able to divorce Ted. Then I'd taken new risks with jobs in public relations and development, and now here I was planning to move across the Atlantic to a foreign country where I knew no one but David.

Looking out of the airplane at the craggy, impenetrable mountain peaks of Greenland, I shivered and drew away from the window. I wondered about David. Behind his protestations of love and commitment lay a trail of girlfriends, and I knew well his attraction to younger women, pretty curly-haired blondes, slightly helpless little fawns. A memory of arriving at his flat one morning from an overseas flight and finding behind the washbowl faucets in the bathroom a large gold ring set with fake emeralds and rubies pierced me for a moment. I had picked it up and put it in his desk drawer. I pushed that memory aside. I had to look forward, shake away misgivings; I had made my decision and knew I must relish challenges, accept my bent for risk-taking. I didn't resemble "other people," those friends and family members who moved forward through life in a logical and practical manner. My thoughts wandered from my parents' remarkable marriage to my own search for an abiding love, as the plane carried me back to the place to which I would soon bid farewell.

Polly, her parents and brothers, Ben and Charlie, 1939

# Thoughts across
# the Atlantic

As my parents' eldest child, I'd been the first to test their parental tolerance and deference to a child's wishes. I don't remember overextending my boundaries. Mother and Dad did not spoil us children; they treated us fairly, disciplined us firmly but quietly.

In 1944 I entered the seventh grade at Northrop School, the private girls' school in Minneapolis, and I turned twelve that year at Christmas time. Every day Mother was busy caring for my brothers and baby sister, running the household, the Red Cross, and her garden. And when my father came home from the office, she gave him her full attention. After he hung his coat and hat in the downstairs closet, he strode to the pantry for the drinks tray and ice, calling to Mother, "I'm on my way to the library, the ice is melting." That meant she should join him immediately. He called the shots.

Mother cut my pigtails and passed along my puffed-sleeved dresses to my sister, CC, but not before one final session of formal family photographs. I could barely smile, I felt so embarrassed wearing those childish clothes. CC was adorable in her Swiss cotton dress with the smock-stitched bodice.

"Pol, a big smile, just once. I promise we'll go to Young Quinlan's after school next week to find a dress for dancing school," Mother said in her clear, but never raised, voice. Her puckered frown revealed her determination. The professional

Polly and her sister, CC, 1944

photographer checked his light meter and readjusted the camera's lens to capture this family composition. My father stood behind Mother seated in a straight-backed chair. She held my sister in her lap while I stood next to her and my brothers, Ben and Charlie, flanked her other side.

"That's it, Bloopie," Dad said as he backed away from the group. "That's enough. Surely Mr. Freden has gotten one good shot." Bloopie was my father's nickname for Mother. It seemed to me like a special code between them. They never argued, but if a slight hint of tension arose, he summoned that endearment to re-solve it.

We broke away from the pose, and I rushed upstairs to fling off forever the dreaded trappings of childhood and pull on navy cotton trousers and rumpled red pullover.

I liked the prospect of dancing school and the promise of grown-up clothes. Mother and several other Junior High mothers from the private girls' and boys' schools organized Friday evening dance classes at the Woman's Club in Minneapolis. This would be safe territory for their progeny to meet members of the opposite sex from families of similar backgrounds. There I would encounter well-brought-up young men, whose skinny adolescent bodies and chiseled chins resembled their fathers', those successful, trust-worthy men of my parents' acquaintance.

At the mention of dancing school, my heart fluttered. Boys. I couldn't talk to Boys. I could only giggle when confronted with the older brothers of my girlfriends. And I was scared of one friend's bully brother who chased us through his house, jumping out from behind doors, grabbing my shoulders, pulling my hair, and locking me in a closet. No adult in that house corralled this brute. In my house, things ran according to my metronome, and there noise was laughter, teasing never threatened.

And now I had to fret about who would dance with me? I was terrified. I needed my mother's wisdom, guidance, and help.

"Do boys like perfume, Mother?" I asked as she stood in the doorway of my bedroom and I walked, freshly bathed, toweled, and powdered, in my cotton slip to my closet, toward a new red-checked taffeta dress. I loved its sweetheart neckline and the hem below my knees, but my heart was fluttering so fast I needed Mother's help with the buttons, which she nimbly fastened, but then vanished before I could remind her about the perfume.

It was actually cologne, Old Spice cologne. I had tried all the samples at Mr. Manning's drugstore before I selected the one with a pungent scent suggesting an exotic Pacific island. I unscrewed the red bottle cap and sprayed clove-scented drops all over my neck, my shoulders, and the top of my dress. Then I was ready for the boys.

A car horn honked. The Clevelands were driving the car pool that first evening. At the sound of the horn, Mother and Dad put down their martinis and walked to the front door to see me off. I pulled the collar of my tweed coat up around my ears. The autumn air felt cold on my bare neck.

At the Woman's Club ballroom we lined up, girls and boys on either side of the room, and the instructors attempted to teach us the basic steps. Then it was a free-for- all pairings for the first dance. There was Jack Reidhead. As an eighth grader, Jack played football on the Blake School Junior Varsity team and flashed a huge smile without braces. His black hair was straight and shiny, like Clark Gable's, and the thought of dancing with him excited me.

Then, as we moved close, he asked, "What you got on?"

"It's a new dress," I said. "I like red."

"No, the smell." He began to cough. "I can't breathe."

I could feel the flush creeping up my face. Suddenly I felt awful. I missed a beat and and stepped on his foot. I stammered something about Old Spice and Mr. Manning being so nice to me. Jack laughed gently, probably self-consciously, as we continued to master the Magic Step, "one and two and three."

When I told Mother about the Old Spice, she shook her head, "You must have doused yourself after I buttoned you up. How did you leave the house without my smelling you?"

She'd been preoccupied talking to Dad in the library, his sanctuary, a square room just off the living room with bookshelves, floor to ceiling, lining the walls. The afternoon light filtered through two windows behind his favorite chair. Several floor lamps, placed near a sofa and two matching arm chairs, illuminated the room and its rich trove of leather-bound books and the brightly colored dust covers of the newer novels.

My father had begun to collect books during his freshman year at Princeton University. Reading and acquiring classical literature, current fiction and nonfiction, biographies and autobiographies was his intellectual and spiritual hobby. Over the years, first editions of Charles Dickens, Jane Austen, Ralph Waldo Emerson, Henry Thoreau, George Eliot, the Brontë Sisters were joined by translations of Molière, Dante, Cervantes, and Alexander Dumas. The collection was vast as it moved into modern times with first editions of Sinclair Lewis, Ernest Hemingway, F. Scott Fitzgerald, John O'Hara, and John Marquandt. There was poetry on a narrow shelf by the windows. A complete set of William Shakespeare and beautifully bound editions of the Old and New Testaments stood on the bottom shelf by the door.

On weekends I joined him in front of the bookshelves, running my hands over the jackets and smooth leather covers which gave the room its pungent aroma. I asked him questions about the authors, and he told me that he had known Scott Fitzgerald slightly when, in their twenties, they both attended Minneapolis and St. Paul Christmas holiday dances. Dad told me that Fitzgerald drew people to him with his jaunty personality, and when he began to write about St. Paul and the Roaring Twenties, Dad began to collect his novels and short stories. He told me about the gaiety, the lighthearted repartee after World War I, and literary geniuses like Rupert Brooke, Wilfred Owen, Fitzgerald, and Hemingway, who had emerged during that period.

Sitting in his chair, a drink on the small side table and a pile of new and well-read books next to him, my father read every evening. Usually I joined my parents before dinner in the library while they were enjoying their martinis. We talked about the day's activities. I knew my parents were proud of me and my school record. "Do the best you can," they always said, which translated, "We know you'll get the best marks." So I tried hard. I was a good student and popular with my girlfriends and with boys at dancing school. I was the right size, small like most 12- and 13-year-old boys. I knew I was fortunate to be petite, and as one of the boys chose me for his partner and escorted me to the dance floor, I never looked over my shoulder at my taller girlfriends. I felt sad for them; size seemed so important.

Freshman year arrived and Blake school dances. I usually had a date, a young man, equally nervous, who brought a gardenia to pin on my long dress. The pin often plunged into a top bit of bosom under my collar bone, and by evening's end the blossom was waxy yellow. Still, like the other girls I mounted these trophies on cardboard and pasted them into my scrapbook.

Throughout my teenaged years, protected and uncertain, I covered up a lack of confidence with giggles and short bursts of rebellious behavior, arguing fruitlessly with my parents about curfews. They did not allow raised or contradicting voices, and I knew my efforts at logic were useless.

Mother always spoke firmly without a quaver in her voice, and she would admonish me harshly if I spoke back; then she would march out of the dining room. Silence followed until she returned and settled into her chair to plunge a fork into the apple crisp topped with whipped cream, and into a conversation muted to suit her decorum.

She'd smile as if nothing had happened and say, "Well, let's hear about the volleyball game, Pol," and dutifully I would reply with an account of the Junior High game against St. Margaret's.

But Mother would be eyeing Dad, catching his attention with a flick of her eye as he took his final bite of apple crisp.

"Time for the music, Benton," she would say, putting down her fork and carefully folding her napkin beside her plate. She ate heartily and quickly as if to jump start her metabolism, converting solid meals into sustainable energy to fuel her next activity.

"Let's play some of those tangos and rumbas, that South American rhythm is catchy," she might say, standing up from the table, pushing away her chair, her feet enclosed in canvas shoes with wedge heels. She would move lightly to imaginary rhythms, leading us all into the living room where she turned switches, activating the lights and the Magna Vox. Her 78 records sat on a shelf within the mahogany phonograph case, and she selected Xavier Cugat and his band recorded from the Copacabana Club in New York City. As each heavy twelve-inch record slapped down on the turntable, we would hold our breath, expecting a crack and crumble, but Mother would take Dad's hand, and he would wrap her in his arms, and bobbing and laughing, they dipped and swirled over the carpet, caught up in their own magic.

A cord fastened my parents to each other. Their personal strands were braided into one enduring embrace. They disagreed only on political party affiliation, and that was because of heritage. Dad, a Democrat, came from a strong Virginia Quaker background on his mother's side, while Mother was from hardy New England stock who were decidedly Republican capitalists.

But that was a minor discord. Their bond, this link, was evident in their body language, not with effusive hugging and kissing but simple, direct eye contact. As one spoke and one replied, their warm, attentive, understanding eyes would remain fastened to each other, not laser-beam sharp, but rich, warm, colorful, soft, like a ribbon.

They were together within a circle, and it was up to them to reach out for us, their children. Their restraint was palpable. We sensed a mysterious chemistry which we could not decipher or diagram. As children we sensed their communion as well as the distance that separated us from them.

Mother's voice was even and resonant while her mother-in-law, my grandmother Gangy, spoke in a high-pitched raspy tone. Mother always cautioned us to speak from our diaphragms, never from our noses. She praised her own mother's beautiful voice, and told us of the recitals and concerts this grandmother had given while she was in her twenties.

Mother seemed the celebrator, devising suitable ways to bring out the best in Dad, not to control, but to protect and enhance. Mother yielded, compromised, and conceded. After her marriage she gave up fishing and hunting trips to the Canadian Rockies with her father and siblings since my father didn't care for hunting or fishing. She hung framed photographs of these Canadian trips in their bedroom.

As a couple they traveled only to the familiar places—New York City, Boston, and the Hillsboro Club on Florida's east coast. Until my father conquered his fear of airplane travel in the early 1960s, they rode trains back and forth across the country. During their New York visits Dad restricted Mother to a day's visit to her sisters in New Haven, a day organized to fit his ritual martinis. He hired a chauffeur with a black limousine to drive them up the Merritt Parkway to Connecticut for martinis and lunch, and then the chauffeur drove them back to Manhattan.

But in my childhood, in our gray clapboard house on the hill above Wayzata and Lake Minnetonka, so sunny and shiny, smelling of Johnson's furniture wax, new tennis balls hanging in mesh bags in the front hall closet, and the blossoms of Mother's prized French lilacs bordering the driveway, my father seemed youthful, energetic, and responsive to new ideas.

We ate our meals at the antique Sheraton table in the bay window of the dining room. Our voices were calm, and we laughed at Dad's simple stories of his day downtown. We carefully cut our chicken breasts, spooned in the mashed potatoes and peas, and relished our cook's delicious pastry treat before our parents' eyes fixed on one another, and the music began to the rhythm of the tango.

I wondered if ever I could love someone the way Mother and Dad loved each other. I thought of love as a fairy tale, Prince Charming appearing magically and sweeping me off my feet, bathing me in love and compassion and gentle care, forever. How was this to happen? From dancing school and Blake dances to marriage? It felt a distant goal.

When I especially liked a boy, my heart began to beat a bit faster, my tummy oddly fluttered. During the summer after high school graduation I found my first boyfriend after an evening's sailboat race, a first kiss, a furtive moment under the sail cover, searching for each other's sticky lips. Up close, it was sweet and glandular. His breath on my face, oddly spicy, surely sprang from a deep well of anxiety and awareness. I felt pleasure and confusion. This sensation was strange. What next? That moment was over, but in my naive way, I had discovered a taste of joy.

How did any of us progress from these childish experiences to courtship and marriage? I'm not sure, but somehow that happened. For me it happened one week after my twentieth birthday, the day after Christmas, It was 1952, and I cast aside my college education to marry Eben. I was head over heels in love but without a clue about how to forge a friendship with a man. As Eben and I moved from Air Force base to base, my husband's fellow second lieutenants became my friends. I felt safely secure, confident I would not foster sexual misunderstandings. I relished the attention of these men, and I returned their humor and confidences. Our times together were lighthearted and generous, and several years after we'd married, now with two sons, Charlie and Chris, Eben and I moved our family back to Minneapolis.

We bought a house in a new development in Wayzata, a bungalow with two stories on the back side overlooking a small pond. I decorated the house while Mother surveyed the bare landscape and began to plant apple, birch, and maple trees, cotoneasters and honeysuckles. I had already discovered I had no "green thumb," so I appreciated her expertise and efforts. When I wasn't caring for the boys, I volunteered at Planned Parenthood or the children's ward at St. Barnabas Hospital. Sometimes I wondered why I employed a babysitter to take care of my own children while I drove fifteen miles and back to care for ill children of strangers. But each time I read to a child or lifted him or her to

Polly and Eben Dobson, December, 1952

Polly, Eben, Chris, Michael, and Charlie, 1959

a more comfortable position, or spooned puréed vegetables into his tiny mouth, I felt hope and gratitude, and returned home to scoop my healthy ones into my arms, and the questions drifted away.

Eben's office was located on the outskirts of downtown Minneapolis, only a twenty-minute car ride from our neighborhood, and so he and I did what I'd always imagined doing. We settled into a life of parenting, community activity, and recreation with our families and friends, and in early December 1958 we celebrated the birth of another son, Michael.

Ours was a marriage founded on shared love and the promises of a good life, just like the lives of our parents and friends, and I felt I'd reached a pinnacle of happiness.

But something must have been missing because when our marriage was threatened, I discovered I couldn't talk to Eben.

Even after seven years of marriage, we did not possess the tools for reasonable discussion. I could only cry and shout and he could only turn away. Something was missing, but I didn't know what that something was. I thought of Mother and Dad bound with their colorful ribbon. That was it. I felt no ribbon. I saw sharp glances and felt constraint, and I didn't know how to reach out, to ask what was wrong or what we could do to find each other? Where was my true friend? I wonder still if the heart of friendship—a frank, honest, no-holds-barred friendship—had ever existed. A true deep relationship might have solved our problems, might have prevented our divorce. But of course I'll never know if that was so.

My second marriage to Ted Brown promised a bustling, active household with stepchildren and a solid banker-husband. But no. Ted and I drew apart, he rooted in conservatism and tradition, and I seeking liberal ideas and spontaneous joys. Once again, this time in 1978 after eleven years, I walked out of a divorce court, sad, disappointed but grateful for my sons' friendship and enduring love, and the work I so enjoyed at the Guthrie Theater. I took a week's holiday each autumn to London to attend the theater and occasionally meet new directors or actors. And now London offered a link to the land of my forebears, and then to one more treasure.

# To David

Over Labor Day weekend, 1984, the children gathered, Charlie and his wife, Juli, from a few miles away in Orono, Chris and his wife, Lisa, from Petaluma, California, and Michael from Los Angeles. They had come to help me sort and divide my possessions between their three households.

My mother was also with us, as a benevolent influence and to watch over her great-grandchildren, Claire, Megan, and Charlie, Jr., sound asleep in his baby carry-cot. My sister, CC, arrived to look over my photo albums and scrapbooks. There would be no room in David's small London flat for extra baggage from past years.

My living room was teeming with family noise and confusion, as I prepared to move to London to live with David.

Sofas, chairs, and coffee tables, removed from their careful arrangement, bore tags noting new owners. The mahogany dining-room table was covered with silver platters, bowls, cutlery, and crystal goblets, wine glasses and champagne flutes, several sets of pottery. Wedgwood and Lenox dinner sets were stacked on the sideboard. Tablecloths, mats, and bed linens were piled on other tables. The bookshelves were bare, stripped of their leather-backed volumes along with current history and biography. They were stacked in piles on the floor.

My sons and daughters-in-law circled joyfully through this collection with no sign of disappointment if an item didn't go their way. I pointed out pieces of china and crystal that had been presents to celebrate my marriage to their father thirty-two years ago; now they would have a new family home. I tried to make sure that each family's new possessions were equal to the others. So I saved for myself a fine French desk and some special china and books to store at my parents' house.

As family tagged and talked, joked and laughed, I looked over at Megan hugging her cousin Claire. Almost the same age, one going on two. And the pleasure of family warmed me.

Into the room my sister carried three leather photo albums. I assured her that as these contained photos of trips over the years to England and Scotland, I would store them. Here was the white album with Eben and my wedding pictures, a keeper.

"Boys, here's what we looked like. Look at my veil, falling off my head," I said, remembering my fine straight hair. Someone had laced together a clutch of bobby pins to hold the heirloom veil in place at least through the church service. I gave the album to Charlie, my eldest son.

I walked to the fireplace to light kindling and a birch log. The blaze leapt, and Chris looked at me.

"What's that for? It's almost eighty degrees outside."

"I have stuff to burn," I said as I marched into my bedroom. I came back with a stack of yellowing envelopes containing letters of past years, embarrassing now to contemplate, sentiments from strange, temporary boyfriends. I tossed them into the flames. "Gone forever, and not soon enough," I said.

CC held up an album from my second marriage. "You're not going to keep these photos, Pol? I won't let you," she said. I could remember the good times without the albums, so I let CC toss them into several plastic garbage bags for removal. I moved to my bedroom again for a box of letters and some curly-edged photos.

"Mom, maybe one of us wants to see those," someone called.

"Oh, no you don't." I smiled. "There they go forever." I laughed at the fire and the flames, at years of baggage that didn't

Polly's grandchildren, Charlie, Claire, and Megan, with her mother, Polly Case, 1984

deserve another moment of daylight, this simple act destroying the detritus of my mistakes, and as they burned I looked over at Mother still sitting calmly on a couch, her arms around her great-granddaughters. She smiled and nodded her approval. Saying goodbye to Mother would be hard. My father was a silent companion now. Suffering from hardening of the arteries and small strokes, he was wheelchair-bound, tended by nurses most of the time. Mother would miss my companionship and support. I knew she was in favor of my decision. She liked David, who over several trips had charmed the family, but I knew she would miss me and my spontaneous visits after work hours or over the weekends.

"Mom, we're going to play some golf now," Charlie said. "We'll be back in time for supper." I thought that was a fine plan, and we talked about meeting at the Woodhill Club, all of us, including Mother. Charlie and Juli's babysitter would care for Claire, as well as Megan and Charlie, Jr. Juli and Lisa left to shop, Mother departed for her house, and CC and I shared a hug.

I sat down to contemplate the last months since my return from Tenerife. I had talked with my children, my parents, my siblings, my friends, and my colleagues at the Humphrey Institute. Each person gave me support, though tinged with a wistful sadness that I would be leaving the community, but I knew I could not move abroad without planning to visit at least twice a year. Keeping in touch with my aging parents and my children on the West Coast was essential. My siblings, Ben and CC, would help Mother manage my parents' household. My brother Charlie had moved to California, but he tried to visit from time to time, and David had agreed to accompany me to the U.S. when he could.

I stood in my living room surrounded by boxes and albums sorted from those for storage and the ones I would take to London with photos from a nurtured childhood, early married days, my babies, and the community activity that had challenged me outside the home. I looked at my school and college photos—what a funny hairdo—and remembered working hard to achieve the best marks and meet my parents' expectations in order to overcome the stabs of homesickness. The last box held my father's *The Sparkers*, his wartime newsletters. I thought of fledgling writing efforts.

I think it was during the summer of 1942, at the height of the War, when I began to write, perhaps because my father wrote a weekly newsletter to those of his employees serving in the Armed Forces. In the four-page missive, he reported on events taking place at the office and in the community. He also told a few funny stories. He was my inspiration. My newspaper also would be a patriotic effort designed to inform neighbors of our victory gardens and Dad's beekeeping venture, of air raid wardens' meetings, and Red Cross bandage-rolling sessions.

I named my newspaper *The Dame Paper* to distinguish it from my father's, which he called *The Sparker*.

For Christmas that year, my parents gave me a child's type-writer with rubber keys. I placed two pieces of carbon paper be-tween three sheets of plain white paper and began typing with two fingers sharply hitting each key for a firm imprint. Tap, slap, the stories began to take shape, and I repeated the process six times for six copies. I then walked to each neighborhood door to personally deliver *The Dame*.

I loved writing about my father, the honey-maker. I think now he might have buried the disappointment he felt over being 4-F by pouring his energy into writing his employee newsletter and producing honey. As a substitute for rationed sugar, honey was a patriotic product, so Dad read instructive manuals, ordered equipment and protective clothing, and set up four hives in our backyard under the apple trees. He had no farming experience. I smiled as I remembered Dad poring over dozens of bee catalogs looking to select the right Queen, and those regal matriarchs that traveled by train in special wire mesh cages from faraway places like Baltimore and Savannah to the depot in Wayzata. Upon arrival the Great Northern station manager hastily tele-phoned Dad at his office to ask him to collect the Queen that evening as he left the commuter train. Dad would let Mother know he was collecting the Queen, so I was on the platform to greet my father and his parcel and walk up the hill to our place.

While Dad changed clothes, I stood guard beneath the ap-ple trees. Soon he was back, dressed in his khaki overalls, with white cotton spats wrapped around his ankles and strapped around his shoes to keep the bees from flying up his pant legs. He wore long canvas cotton gloves and a big khaki cloth hat with a heavy veil that fastened under his chin; whenever it wasn't fastened se-curely, hostile bees crawled in and stung him. And when that hap-pened, he couldn't trap them with those awkward, stiff gloves. Poor Dad wound up with many stings.

But that first day, as I recalled, he was ready to install the Queen into her hive. He carefully opened the top of the hive that teemed with worker and drone bees, then lifted the Queen's box, pulling out a small cork from the bottom that revealed a wall of sugar protecting Her Majesty.

Catching a whiff of her, the worker bees quickly gathered to eat the sugar, and Dad replaced the top of the hive. Now the matriarch was in command of her family, the hive was abuzz, and moments later my typewriter was humming with the latest news.

On weeknights and each weekend Dad tended his hives, and by summer's end, he was ready to extract the golden honey, an all-out effort. Saturday morning several fellow hardware company employees would come over to join Dad in setting up the heavy metal extraction drum and turning the pipe-like crank. From each hive they then gently removed waxy trays and placed them, four at a time, in the extractor which they speedily whirled. Taking turns twisting the crank, the men chortled as the heavy liquid sloshed around inside the shrieking machine.

And then the gift appeared—golden apple or amber clover honey poured through a spout out into a huge container. The men checked for obvious impurities as they decanted the honey into glass jars. I pasted on the bright red and yellow labels: "From the Apiary of Benton Case." Dad gave away most of his honey to family and friends.

Mother had begun her own "war effort" several months after Pearl Harbor. She was a Home Service officer of the Minneapolis branch of the Red Cross. Wearing a handsome blue uniform and cap, she gave a full day each week to this volunteer work, assisting families who needed help and information about their men and women in service. If there was a family emergency, Mother contacted the service person and his superior officer to request a home leave.

For *The Dame Paper* I recorded Mother's most exciting days as she was assigned to round up soldiers or sailors who were AWOL. She stalked Washington Avenue, not far from Dad's store in Minneapolis, where these servicemen gathered in dark, smoky bars. On those nights Mother would arrive at the supper table slightly flushed, her eyes sparkling from a successful roundup, and

I'd run from the table for a pencil and piece of paper, and Mother's luring some poor soldier from a dark, mysterious bar would be my big story for the week.

She and another Red Cross volunteer had entered the Persian Palms bar and walked through the rooms looking for Private Haskins. They asked each soldier his name, and behind the jukebox they had found Private Haskins. Mother said he burst into tears when they told him he was AWOL and that his mother was worried sick about him. They escorted the soldier to the local Red Cross office where they phoned his reporting officer and his family. Shaking her head Mother said these young men knew they must fight but they were terrified.

Dad would look up from his dinner plate just about then, smile at Mother and say something like, "I wish I'd known you were lunching at the Persians Palms, I'd have walked down from the store and joined you." And Mother's face would brighten, and she'd laugh as she always did when Dad teased her.

And so I had my headline: POLLY CASE CAPTURES PRIVATE HASKINS. (She was "Polly" too.)

*The Dame Paper* had a life of two years, covering several growing cycles of our victory gardens, frequent dog fights, and my parents' war efforts.

As the eldest child I had commanded attention and it fueled my ambition and desire to succeed. My parents had given me confidence and direction, and as I looked over my albums and photos, the scrapbooks filled with war photos and news items, I realized how drawn I'd always been to the larger world—the world beyond the prairie. These memorabilia were precious, connecting me to my identity, my heritage, and they were signs, too, signs in some way of the new directions on which I was likely to embark.

And then it was time. Election day, 1984, my departure day for London. Walter Mondale was unlikely to beat Ronald Reagan, a favorite to win a second term. First I cast my vote for Mondale, and then stopping at the gas station to fill my tank before my last work day and the sale of my car to a friend, I shed my first tears. There

Arrival at Gatwick Airport, U.K., November, 1984

was Tony Feser, gas station attendant, party bartender, and longtime
family friend. As I signed a credit card receipt inside the station, I
fell into Tony's arms, snuggling against his rough gabardine jacket.
Mindful of that embrace, on my return visits we would hug each
other each time he filled my gas tank or, at a party, my wine glass.

That night, as I flew over Nova Scotia, the pilot announced
that Reagan had won a second term, a landslide victory against
Mondale. I thought of my parents who would, like me, be disappointed. After years of listening to her husband, Mother had
finally joined him as a Democrat. Years earlier I had lost faith in
the Republicans' lack of compassion for the people. And then I
looked ahead. Political conversations in London would be interesting; David and most of his friends were Tories, ardent support-
ers of Margaret Thatcher, and David revered Reagan, who refused
to give an inch to the Russians. All of this awaited me. But I knew
I was ready.

# Cracking the Code

As Northwest Airline Flight 45 touched down at Gatwick airport, I swallowed hard. I was here in London for the rest of my life, no longer a visitor, here to live with David in his tiny bachelor's flat. How romantic my decision to change the course of my life to follow my heart, but I was still breathless from the whirl of going-away parties and farewells at home, friends squealing, "How can you resign from Woodhill?" That was our country club where for over thirty years I had played tennis and golf, swam, drunk gin and tonics and white wine, eaten countless meals, danced to the brassy sounds of live orchestras. And Woodhill was where Eben and I had celebrated our wedding reception. I hadn't realized how hard saying goodbye would be, but now all that was a glow of memory. I was excited, tired, anxious. Too late for doubts. The pilot taxied to the gate and doors opened to the British customs official welcoming us passengers to the U.K. As I pulled my two luggage carts heaped with possessions through Customs, David waved and took out his camera to document my arrival.

Then I catapulted into my new life.

In the beginning there were two Londons—the city of work with its hectic days, gray pinstriped suits and black walking shoes, and the society with its elegant evenings, black cocktail dresses and shiny stilettos.

David's bachelor flat, Elystan Place

Weekday mornings David and I bathed, ate bowls of breakfast cereal and sipped our coffee as we dressed. Then we set off for work. David often drove me to the South Kensington underground station. I could have walked the eight blocks, but he was eager to ease the journeys. Days I worked to establish the Humphrey Institute/U.K. office, evenings I accompanied David, joyfully if nervously. I met his myriad friends. We attended dinner parties, dances, concerts, and plays; dinners at the large homes and small flats of our friends, guests elegantly attired in black and dark suits or informally in slacks and sports jackets. Most hosts prepared and served the meal without cook or butler.

So there I was, the village girl from the middle of the U.S. for the first time hitting the big city. In Minnesota I drove the freeways on automatic pilot and retraced my route homewards. I couldn't do this in London with its web of underground and bus transport. Now I faced daily choices the moment I stepped from our front door. Which mode of transport or foot path would be the most efficient? And the choices and changes both exhilarated and overwhelmed.

Bill Bowman, the most active member of the HHHI/U.K. Committee, arranged an office for me, a tiny room in the basement of Robert Hyde House in Bryanston Square, just a few blocks north of Marble Arch and around the corner from his office. It was a central location, a space where I could make contacts with staff of other non-profits in the building. To reach this office and those located in the financial district, the City of London, or in Whitehall, the heart of Parliament and government buildings and some of the organizations on the periphery of London, I rode the underground. And because I was introducing HHHI to public affairs institutions and civil service officers, I was traveling everywhere. Each appointment, each interview led to yet another neighborhood, and so within weeks I knew my way around the city. Soon after that I began taking day trips to universities and institutions around the country—Manchester, Southampton, Oxford, and Cambridge—and my world grew still larger.

In the evenings, I told David tales of my days and he offered his opinion that many Brits think Americans take themselves too seriously, that many of us use ponderous, complicated language. He said he was excited about what I was doing but warned me not to offer details of my public affairs work; our friends, he said, simply wouldn't care. He explained they loved my being here but didn't need to know exactly what I was doing. I tried to understand this world, so different from the one I'd known all my life.

I stopped talking and began to watch and listen. That is, I remained quiet until someone did ask me to explain the Humphrey Institute and my role. Then I'd eagerly begin. He or she almost always responded by telling me that my position sounded "frightfully highpowered," a British phrase for a lofty, complex job, something beyond quick comprehension. I accepted this term as a veiled compliment and chose to simplify the repartee. After some weeks I began to grasp this different work style. We Americans embraced challenge and issues and actions to resolve. In some ways we were compulsive; at least I knew I was, eager to solve and move forward. In London the process was layered, reasoned, options weighed and reweighed before a solution was found. I thought back to my father's discussions at our dinner table during my childhood and remembered how he and his contemporaries had dealt with business and community problems. They were not afraid to make new acquaintances and offer them positions in their companies. The British elite, in contrast, seemed secure in their own circles.

Life around our village green bridged the two Londons, and it was here I began to feel most at home. Daily I connected with the friendly vendors and shopowners. Each London neighborhood was a village, a combinations of houses, apartments, and public housing buildings clustered around a village green, a triangle or square of grass and a few trees surrounded by the shops. Ours seemed a marvelously colorful place with our green grocer offering tulips, daffodils, lilies, heather, sweet William, hyacinths, and pots of violets, and seasonal and imported vegetables, shiny magenta aubergine, dark green courgettes, and garlic knobs strung like Christmas lights over the awning. And there was the butcher shop, its proprietor in fresh white overalls and cap sharpening his knives or cutting slabs of beef or pork, weighing strings of British sausage or plucking wild game. At the ironmonger's I recalled childhood Saturdays in my father's wholesale store, and there was the chemist who, from behind his counter, gazed over shelves of emollients, body cleansers, and pain killers and brewed his own cough syrup, a licorice-tasting brown liquid that reminded me of the medicine I'd taken as a child. Our pub was a magnet for the local dwellers; canned music wafted from beneath its doors, and during a football game shouts and cheers drifted out onto the Green. The Pakistani news agent stocked tobaccos, magazines, sweets, and crisps alongside U.K. and foreign newspapers, and Rose, our laundress, greeted me twice a week, when I delivered on my way to work two sailing bags filled with our laundry and after work collected neatly folded clothes and bed coverings. At Christmas time, Rose baked and served tiny mince pies and glasses of sherry to her clientele. I never cared for sherry, but I did love the celebration and happily nursed a glass and nibbled at the pie, as I learned to love being part of this world.

Every evening at 5:45 P.M. precisely, the sky overhead exploded with the sound of the Concorde taking off for the U.S., and on spring and summer mornings we woke to a dawn chorus, the tiny songbirds hovering in the courtyard fruit trees behind our flat and around the Green singing their hearts out. Inside our flat and inside those of our friends, silver and crystal gleamed on dinner tables, each place set with at least three forks, knives, and spoons to support each course. Hosts poured champagne, Veuve Clicquot or Perrier Jouet at the drop of a hat, no special occasion needed.

Within a month of my arrival I no longer dreaded the darkness of autumn and winter, those days when the sky was dark by 4 P.M. I would emerge to the darkness from my basement office in Bryanston Square and catch a bus at Marble Arch down Park Lane to the Piccadilly line and the tube to the South Kensington station. I walked home down Elystan Street and up the steps of our building to the outside gallery to behold our lighted kitchen windows. As I turned the key, music poured from the door and lights blazed. David spared no kilowatts. The phone could be ringing, and there might be something brewing on the stove, or at least there would soon arise a lively conversation about whose turn it was to produce tonight's dinner.

It was then that I must have remembered the dreaded darkness, icy cold, and blowing snow of Minnesota winters. London was mild, in spite of rain and wind; the temperature rarely dropped below thirty-two degrees, zero to the Brits who couldn't comprehend my tales of Minnesota temperatures that in January often plummeted well below zero.

At our front door, I turned my key into the lock and pushed the door. "Hello, hello." "Hello, Darling, there you are. Had a good day?" David would be there, folding me in his arms and giving me a big kiss. The welcome, an all-season welcome, offering comfort, light, and warmth.

In previous years I had dreaded the onset of winter's dark mornings and evenings. In November 1961, when Eben and I divorced, our boys were young—Charlie seven, Chris five, and Michael not yet three. I had buried my loneliness in mothering—breakfast, preparations for school, activities with Michael who was not yet in school, afternoon homework and supper and washing up for bed. After they had fallen asleep, I closed my bedroom curtains to conceal the mounds of snow and harsh winds raging through the pine trees. I let our poodle, Percy, out the front door for one final pee, but he always made quick work to return to the warmth.

For me in those days, darkness hovered. That first year, and subsequent years, at Christmas time we all missed Eben's joyful spirit, and his Christmas Eve last-minute shopping sprees, flinging thrift to the winds and buying me extravagant jackets, skirts, and dresses like the beautiful red lace evening gown he gave me the Christmas just after Michael's birth. I longed for the sight of those long pink boxes from Harold's, the ladies' store in Minneapolis which catered to the anxieties of young husbands who had waited until the last moment to find gifts for their wives; and I ached not to feel excitement I'd always felt as I untied the ribbons and dived through tissue paper to find the treasures within. I felt too the way the boys missed Eben's infectious presence. Their father and his new wife, Sonia, and their daughter, Ellen, had moved to California.

When I married Ted the darkness wasn't relieved. A house full of our combined families and mounds of presents under the tree never restored my spirit or helped me embrace Ted's routine and tradition. Each year he gave me a pin, a gold circle holding a bird or garnished with semi-precious stones that glittered but didn't resonate. I always thanked him, pinned it on my jacket, and a month later placed it in my top drawer under my hankies.

And then came the darkness of the second divorce. Then I was truly alone. The boys were in college, I left for work in winter dawn darkness, often staying in town late after work, attending courses at Metro State University or meeting friends for a play or concert. But now, at long last, I was celebrating a winter of joy and light.

I did love my new world, though that first year, as Thanksgiving drew near, I began to feel homesick. That holiday, a normal London workday, I was sitting in my basement office listening to the cockney voices of several workmen repairing the central skylight in our building. Waiting until mid-afternoon to span the time difference between London and the U.S., when I would make my phone calls, I watched the clock until at last it was time and I heard the voices of my children and mother. Suddenly I felt far away, isolated, beyond their warm embrace. I forced my voice to sound cheery as I described my two Londons, and I listened closely as they told me of the Thanksgiving gatherings they would enjoy later that day. I could feel my heart growing heavy with sadness.

After work that Thanksgiving, on the underground platform, I stepped around a bedraggled young woman squatting in a corner hiding from approaching trains; she held a tiny baby wrapped in a soiled bunting. She looked up at me and whispered, "Milk for my baby?" She reached out a hand clutching a cup. I dug into my bag and pulled out some coins, wishing somehow to comfort this sad young mother, wanting to give her an American hug. But English people don't hug. English people greet each other smiling, offering first one cheek and then the other for a quick peck, doing so without touching any other part of the body, no shoulder squeeze or touch of an arm, a sort of sparrow peck. I suddenly ached for the warmth of American hugs.

Still, I shoved aside the clouds of homesickness and also those other clouds that sometimes arose—insecurity. David's old girlfriends were part of our social circle, and sometimes I worried about their presence. Though I wished I could, I couldn't sweep away these fears the way I could so easily blow away tiny bits of unfamiliar black soot from our open windowsills.

Deep inside I harbored distant memories—fears of loves fading and lost. I could never forget that moment at a summer dinner party in 1959 when I discovered Eben and Sonia alone in our hosts' living room gazing at each other with a newfound passion. Now, whenever I heard David chatting on the phone with Sheila, Sally, or Jill, making a lunch or cocktail plans, I would grab a jacket from our closet and leave the flat for a spontaneous errand I simply had to do at that moment. Outside I would meander for a few blocks pushing away my feelings of insignificance, believing I was just David's American girlfriend who had transferred her life and all her chattels across the Atlantic to perch in his tiny bachelor flat. A fool.

Whenever David invited Sheila, Sally, or Jill for dinner or when, on occasion, we visited their homes, I felt wary. I could feel the atmosphere shifting slightly as David and the old girlfriend exchanged stories of past days, smiled conspiratorially about this or that memory—the time they lost their way to the wedding in Surrey and drove around in circles missing the ceremony, or sailing into Poole Harbour without the engine and gently nudging the pier, or the downpour at Glyndebourne just as they spread out the picnic—bantering about events of which I had no knowledge. I tried to reassure myself; why, I asked silently, should I care about their memories? Better if he met them alone for lunch or a drink, I felt, for then I wouldn't have to endure the insecurity that washed over me as I observed those intimate moments.

I loved David's three daughters, Benedetta (Bino), Virginia (Niotti), and Talia. The eldest two were married with families and lived close by. Talia, almost thirty years old, lived by herself. I was busy at work so I asked her, between her secretarial jobs, to type and file for me two days a week. I liked her company, her light chuckle filling the empty room. As we prepared for the first meeting of my Board, I laid out documents and background materials for the members, and Talia duplicated and prepared neat folders with tabbed sections for each subject.

At the meeting he was chairing, Hector Laing, chairman of United Biscuits and personal friend of Margaret Thatcher, lifted my folder and shook his head. "What is this?" he thundered. "I

David's daughters, Talia, Virginia, and Benedetta

wanted one sheet of paper. What is all this?" Laing shook his head at me, but I had no answer. From across the table, Bill Bowman glowered at me, unable to conceal his anger. Or was that embarrassment he felt? Laing was his former boss.

After the others departed, Bill yelled at me for assuming an American board meeting practice would be correct in London. I had failed my first test. I swallowed tears as I walked from the meeting to the Green Park underground station. I called David from a public phone and burst into tears.

"You'll be home soon and we'll go to the Heywoods' for supper. Forget about those brutes," he said. The sound of his voice comforted me. I looked forward to the evening and to forgetting.

After several glasses of Ben Heywood's champagne, the anguish began to ease, and my tongue was lubricated. Before I could stop myself I burst forth with my story, painting the incident as an amusing one. I'd come to understand that's what the British liked, the light touch. David and the Heywoods offered understanding, but they took more pleasure in the rendition.

The next day Bill apologized for his rudeness, and we wrote up the minutes of the meeting to promptly assure the Board that we were indeed on the right track. I had overcome the first work obstacle.

But that was nothing compared to an obstacle within the social scene. Clothes. Before I left Minnesota I bought a new evening dress to wear at a London Christmas charity ball. It was the latest fashion with spaghetti straps, a low-cut soft purple satin with a petal shaped skirt. Elegant, I thought, until I noticed David's critical eye as I dressed. He said nothing, but I could feel his disapproval, and when we arrived at the Savoy Hotel, I quickly saw my mistake. English women wore bell-shaped long skirts and bodices with puffed sleeves to the elbow. English women sported glittering diamond necklaces and pearl chokers fastened with diamond and ruby clips. I fingered my single strand of cultured pearls and shivered in my flimsy costume, miserable until the four-course dinner ended, and we began to dance.

David took me in his arms, placing his hand firmly across my bare back and guiding me comfortably around the dance floor. I no longer felt out of place as we danced to familiar tunes, those "Big-Band" pieces of Benny Goodman and Tommy Dorsey, traditional American music. I forgot about buying a ball gown, I didn't care or have the time for shopping. I would, I decided, just be myself.

As that first London Christmas drew near, David sensed my longing for my family, and it was he who proposed we both fly to Minneapolis for the holiday. I hadn't realized how deep my homesickness was until his suggestion. I was overjoyed. We arrived in Minneapolis in time for a party at Charlie and Juli's house where I reached for my granddaughter, Megan, and swung her around the living room. She giggled and hugged me tightly.

That visit we stayed with my parents. Every morning as David passed by my father's bedroom, he would chorus, "Good Morning, Benton. Have a good night?" I'm certain that Dad, by now unable to talk, heard the lusty English voice. David would then stop by Dad's bed and give his arm a squeeze, and Dad would intently look at David. We all believed that this was Dad's way of saying thank you, and Mother told me how much she appreciated David's treating Dad as if he could converse.

Indeed light had returned to my world. That trip one icy morning as we dressed, David pulled out a small package from his suitcase. I knew from the size and shape it was a jewelry box. Inside I found a lovely pearl and garnet necklace, the necklace I had liked so much at a friend's jewelry exhibition. I held the beads up to the light. I loved garnets with their rich old-fashioned dark red color. "This is the necklace I loved," I said, and David smiled and said, "Yes," and then as I fastened the clasp and patted the beads, he said quietly, "I think we should get married."

I looked up to see him grinning from ear to ear and holding out his arms. "The grandchildren would like it if we did," he whispered against my cheek.

I had no doubts. I nodded as tears filled my eyes, laughed when David told me we weren't fooling the grandchildren or anybody, for that matter. It was time, and he was ready. He loved living with me, I seemed to love London life and the future was ours, together.

"Are you ready?" he asked.

I thought about the recent months; I had followed my heart and now I knew I could never return to the Midwest and admit "it hadn't worked," that I didn't have the right stuff to make a life change, that I couldn't accept British ways, couldn't laugh about my dowdy summer clothes, hadn't the courage to set a new course.

Failure wasn't me.

And there was more than that. I loved David. I loved the excitement of London life, the life he had asked me to share. Yes, the American girlfriend could become the wife, his wife. Those others? They would be plain old "past girlfriends." I had earned new credentials. And as David that day and often afterwards whispered to me, I had touched his heart. And he held mine.

We returned to London for New Year's Eve, and there we began to prepare for an April wedding. In the light of the new

Polly and David's wedding photo, April 6, 1985, London

year, my two Londons began to merge. David had offered a stamp on my passport that announced to the world that I was a British resident, not a visitor. Now, in the others' eyes, I was legitimate. I could be trusted for the long term. I was not an American working on a short-term project, a visitor who would soon return to her native land. I was, rather, here as a permanent part of British life and society. David had given me a lifetime gift, his love and marriage. Diamonds and rubies were for others. With pride and panache I wore my garnet and pearl necklace, reminding me that my two Londons now formed a single circle.

# Hats in the Air

Often now when I think of David and our years together, glimpses of places and conversations flash through my head and I go to the scrapbooks to find firsthand information. At random, I find a photo or clipping that reminds me of a vivid conversation or event such as this photo from a scrapbook he produced during our early married years.

It was a dark January evening as I returned to the flat. David had spread out his current scrapbook at the square table in our sitting room. I hung up my coat and leaned down beside him, giving him a kiss. He picked up a recent copy of the *Sunday Times* magazine, turned to a page, and clipped a photograph of a delicious-looking supper concoction. I had to admit the photograph was inspiring, a perfect dish after a concert or theater—poached eggs, hollandaise sauce topped with lumpfish caviar. He pasted it onto a blank page and wrote a caption underneath it: "Hats in the Air, enjoyed by one and all."

"What are you doing?" I asked as I leaned over his shoulder. "You haven't made it yet. How can you put that into your scrapbook?"

He turned with the sly smile I was beginning to know so well. "I know that's what'll happen. Can't miss if you follow the recipe."

"Darling," I argued, "that's a bit much. The Thorolds aren't coming until tomorrow night and you haven't even bought the food."

David enjoyed cooking. He told me that after his divorce he knew he had to master some kitchen skills to avoid eating "fish fingers" every night. So friends gave him cookbooks, and he learned the basics, carefully measuring ingredients and following the instructions to a T.

"You can't cook without following directions," he said frequently as he watched me toss in this and that without checking the recipe. Men who like to cook make good chefs, and so it was with David as long as he had full reign in the kitchen.

The next evening when I returned from the office he had begun preparing our dinner. As soon as I took off my coat and stowed my bag, I was ready to set the table. For the dinner parties he planned and cooked, David liked to cover the table with well-worn, bright pink cotton tablecloths, orange and blue placemats, and striped napkins of varying colors. I preferred a more tailored, color-coordinated look, but this evening was his event, so I pulled his favorite cloths from the small black trunk he used as an end table.

"Remember all the forks," he called, a not-so-subtle reminder of English ways; three forks, two knives, and one dessert spoon for a first course, entree, and dessert, a side plate for bread, and three glasses—for water, white and red wine. No scrimping at this table. I also liked to use china that matched, but David liked pottery of mixed designs, so that evening I placed his favorite blue flowered saucers as side plates beside the earthenware pottery dinner plates.

"Is your new dish a first course or the main?" I called. I couldn't be sure because I had learned David often changed his mind at the last minute.

"First, so I can 'relaaax' with the second," he said, stretching the last syllable of relax as he always did with a broad American accent.

"I have a fork and knife for it. Does it need a spoon?" I asked as I placed a pot of lavender violets in the center of the table and moved his newest scrapbook to his desk.

"I hope not. If so, I'll have failed to hold it all together." The center table was the focal point of our living-sitting room, the place we ate every meal, sat to read and talk during the day, and the spot where he frequently worked on his scrapbooks.

David's children and grandchildren, all living within several blocks of us, called in frequently and usually pulled down a book to find their photos or bits of letters or school programs. Sometimes, a grandchild would frown and say something like, "G'Pop, you have more pictures of Jack than me." And then David would make a conscientious effort to balance future pages.

Now he called from the kitchen, "Put out the cashews, but be sure to fill up the bowl. It looks so much better that way." I thought he was preparing too much food, a cold meat and salad platter and then ice cream meringues would follow the egg dish, which was complicated to prepare.

"You know, Darling, you could've just had chicken in the brick—it would do for two courses," I called to him.

"I do that all the time. The Thorolds have had it a million times," he argued.

"But everyone loves it," I said, even though I knew it was too late to shift to chicken. David prepared it differently each time, and each time it was absolutely perfect. The key was the clay brick, well-seasoned from many uses, into which he first placed greens to hold the cooking juices, then chicken, and then piled atop chunks of turnips, onions, potatoes, carrots, shredded parsley and rosemary, lots of cracked pepper, black olives, and crushed juniper berries. He tossed a handful of berries into a plastic bag, whacked the bag with a hammer, smashing the berries to release their aroma, and then sprinkled them into the dish, and covered everything liberally with red wine.

But the real trick was remembering to turn on the oven before we left for the concert so that the dish baked slowly for three hours. On our return, when we walked up the steps of our building and entered our outside gallery, we inhaled a reassuring aroma. The meat would be so tender, nearly falling off the bone, the juices bubbling over the top of the pot. David served the chicken pieces and vegetables in soup plates, and when our guests departed I would place the carcass with the leftover vegetables and a fresh onion into a cooking pot, cover it with water and sherry and boil it into a rich broth.

It was soul-food, and just thinking of it, still, all these years later, makes me feel hungry and warm all over.

When I walked to the kitchen door to see how he was faring, David smiled at me. "You know this all is a breeze when you're retired. When I was working long hours, I'd invite people for eight-thirty, never before, so I had plenty of time to get it all together."

This was a far cry from a midweek dinner party in Minneapolis where people gathered at six or six-thirty.

"I'd come home at six or so with the food, roll up my sleeves, pour a bit of vodka to keep myself company, and take off," David continued, "but after several parties, I gave up the vodka. I sipped as I chopped and stirred and then at dinner I had to pinch myself to stay awake."

I smiled as I remembered my own stifled yawns at our dinner parties. Often as we sipped the dregs of our demitasses, our guests would ask David to open a scrapbook, and I knew this action would postpone their departure for at least an hour. Though I always groaned inwardly, David was delighted when friends hovered over his shoulder as he explained the photos and their succinct and witty entries, and so, as the evening drew on towards midnight, I sat across the room nodding from one guest to the other. Starting to do the dishes would be rude, so I simply learned to smile and make chirpy noises, willing myself to stay awake.

Aside from these late scrapbooking moments, I enjoyed our dinner parties. The conversation was lively, and our friends were well read, informed, and eager to talk. In those late 1980s and 90s they spoke positively about America and Ronald Reagan's aggressive position towards the Russians. The Cold War appeared to be over. Our two countries were marching in step to face new challenges in the Middle East. I deeply appreciated the British attitude, and I felt comfortable with our friends as we discussed politics from all angles. Our Tory friends were dedicated to conservative principles, and their heroes were Margaret Thatcher and John Major, her solid successor. In fact in 1992 David campaigned vigorously for Major's reelection, going door-to-door through North Kensington wards. To our friends, a Labour victory would be a catastrophe, and though I was an American Democrat (and had no vote in the U.K.), I couldn't back the far left British Labourites who led their party. No one trusted Neil Kinnock or Roy Hattersley. The Brits took sides and didn't compromise. As David and I observed and talked politics, I often thought of my parents discussing politics over my childhood dinner table.

For several years, David and I gave a cocktail party in early October for fifty to seventy-five friends at the Royal Thames Yacht Club in Knightsbridge. People were happy to see each other after the summer holidays and to renew acquaintances. We booked a medium-sized private room on the second floor overlooking Knightsbridge or Hyde Park, and the staff would operate a full bar, passing around wine and serving hot and cold hors d'oeuvres. Each year as we planned the event I suggested that we not pack all our friends into that room, but David always replied, "People like to be chock-a-block, hugga-mugga." That was a favorite expression of his, and so it became mine. David felt that close quarters excited people, that they loved it. And so every year we did create hugga-mugga, and if my neck twisted as I looked upward to one tall friend after another, I knew the pain would be only a quick flash, and that always the party would be wonderful.

Our socializing was constant, without let-up, except maybe during August when we usually were sailing. Each autumn the pace ignited: cocktail parties, small dinner parties at friends' houses, Sunday lunches at country houses, concerts, and theater outings. At the same time I was working four days a week, trying to put forth the best image of America both at work and at parties. The British often perceived American economic success as corporate greed, ours a land of money-grubbers who no longer revered tradition and courteous manners. In some small way I thought that, as an educated, sensitive American with a light sense of humor, I might change that belief.

And as time passed, I saw my efforts were working. Former Labour Prime Minister, James Callaghan, chaired the Board of Directors of the U.K. program and invited me often to meet in his office at the House of Commons. I loved entering the Houses of Parliament, skirting the lines of British constituents and tourists patiently waiting for entry. To the entrance guards, I simply said that Jim Callaghan was expecting me and they gave me instant access to those marbled halls.

The HHHI program was growing, and I continued to travel to Manchester, Southampton, Cambridge, East Anglia, and Belfast to attend public affairs events and meet university professors to discuss expanding our reciprocal programs and attend public affairs events. Thanks to my loyal Committee member and mentor, Bill Bowman, I met officers of the U.S./U.K. Fulbright Commission and in 1986, became an American member of the Commission.

It was all heady stuff, but I was tired. For almost two years I kept this pace, but with each month I wished for a break from all the socializing and steady conversation. Conversation was a prized British skill, and often friends put me on the spot asking Reagan's position on the Contras or, later, Bill Clinton's qualifications for the Presidency. Always I tried to provide a reasoned answer, but if I failed to speak quickly enough or answer a question convincingly, someone would interrupt. And at those times I became angry, either suffering in silence or forcing my way into the conversation at the next opportunity. During these encounters, I sometimes felt the fuzzy edges of homesickness. I bit my lip or brushed my hand across my eyes. I didn't want anyone to see my lip quiver. The image of America rode on my shoulders. At least that's how I often felt.

I can't recall exactly how I convinced David that we had to slow down, make some social priorities, but he did come up with a plan, a series of Keep Free Evenings. At the beginning of each month, we would sit down with our respective diaries and deliberately write KF on at least one evening's space each week. The principle of Keep Free was inviolate, though we would pay attention to extraordinary circumstances—an unannounced visit from an out-of-town friend, for instance. Still, both parties had to agree, and over the years our KF evenings were heaven-sent; we would stay in or walk to one of our neighborhood cinemas for an early evening film and then return to the flat to eat supper alone.

Still, David never ceased to relish the formal London dinner party where hosts invited interesting friends who might or might not know the others. I never knew whom to expect when we pressed a doorbell and entered a drawing room. Our host would introduce us to the others as he or she poured a glass of wine or champagne, and we might know one couple of the five assembled or maybe none at all. At first I would feel nervous, not knowing how to begin a conversation although I liked, "What was the highlight of your day?" or "Your favorite holiday this year?" Everyone was on his or her best mettle, so that conversation became lively and stimulating, casting aside talk of illness, domestic troubles, or debilitating gossip. We carried forth on higher planes— politics, higher education, cultural offerings, music, art exhibitions, sporting events, or our favorite sailing adventures.

Anne and Peter Thorold gave wonderful dinner parties, usually eight or ten of us around their table, a mixture of hard-fast Tories and passionate Liberals exchanging views and political prognostications, and there usually would be literary and professional people to add their wisdom to the discussion. Our younger friends, such as Herschel and Peggy Post, always produced a fine party combining corporate executives still working in the City with cultural aficionados—who could be one and the same. And at the Royal Yacht Squadron, David's yacht club at Cowes, weekend guests exchanged sailing stories, cruises around the U.K., Ireland, Normandy and Brittany harbors, and south to the Mediterranean and beyond.

Polly and David sailing on the Beaulieu River, U.K., 1986

But after we devised our KF evenings, at our own dinner parties David and I would share smiles as we watched our guests warming to each other, searching out common interests and pleasures, and when he passed by, he would lean close and whisper, "It's all going so well, we can duck out to the cinema."

Our favorite cinema was the Chelsea Arts on the Kings Road where we enjoyed foreign films. As my passion was theater, we often attended favorite work at the smaller, off-West End venues like the Almeida in north London, where Harold Pinter's work was frequently performed and Pinter might direct or play a major role as in *No Man's Land*, and the Young Vic where we often saw Arthur Miller's work. I remember with deep pleasure the night when Miller attended a performance of *The Price* and sat near us. At the interval, the audience rose to applaud him.

David's love of baroque music led us all over London to churches with natural acoustics such as Spitalfields in east London and St. John's in Smith Square near Parliament.

These were unforgettable moments. David often said that a person could attend a different concert or play each night for months without repeating the event. This was the London I relished, and now as I look at David's scrapbook entries, I smile at colorful photos of food presentations, menus from his Yacht Club on the Isle of Wight, and photos he often took of me sitting at an outdoor restaurant in Italian or French villages during our summer sailing cruises. I remember his command of our kitchen in London, discovering and preparing new recipes to tempt the palates of our friends.

# A Gray Face

A warm breeze from an open window circled through the Fulbright Commission's conference room. On this mid-July afternoon in 1989, four years into our marriage, I was meeting Eleanor Gall, the Fulbright Alumni Association secretary, to discuss autumn projects when suddenly I heard a voice at the doorway. "Polly, you're wanted on the telephone. It's a doctor's office." Doctor's office. After David had dropped me off at the Fulbright office he was meeting Dr. Pigott nearby in Harley Street. I thanked the receptionist and took the call at an extension phone.

"Mrs. Grose, this is Dr. Pigott's nurse. Your husband's blood pressure is very high. The doctor is taking him to the Harley Street Clinic."

I mumbled something and started to shake. Eleanor walked to my side, and when I told her the news, without a word she took my arm to escort me from the office to her parked car. She insisted on driving me the few blocks to the hospital.

I had feared this would happen—I remembered David's words to me six years earlier on my first London visit. "I'm old, older than you think," he said. "I'm sixty-two. You shouldn't get involved." But I had paid no attention.

I thanked Eleanor, left her car, and dashed up the hospital steps to the reception desk, where I learned David was on the second floor in the Intensive Care unit. My stomach lurched, and I started to shake again. Steady, steady. I took the lift and entered the critical care unit.

There was David stretched out on a white bed with Dr. Pigott at his side. He was a pewter gray, clammy gray. His eyes were open.

"Darling, hello, I feel awful." That was all he said.

I leaned towards him. His breath was stale, and he looked anxious, suddenly so tired, so old, this vital person stripped of color. I could see his breastbone rising from a concave chest.

And suddenly I was looking at Dad. It was Dad, this man with the concave chest and putty gray face. David was my Dad.

Here I saw my father, not in London but in a Minneapolis hospital after another collapse. Dad's eyes were closed, he was gray and thin, convulsing. A nurse held him fast, restraining him, but Dad had been ill for at least fifteen years by then, and this was not my father but my beloved husband.

I heard David's voice again in my head. "I'm too old for you. Don't get involved," he had whispered softly that first night in his tiny flat.

Now as I looked at my husband, an old man, gray, clammy, weak and likely dying, lying helpless on a hospital bed in the corner of the IC ward, I felt a rug pulled from beneath my feet. He wore a gray gown. Why not another color? Bright green or yellow. No, that would be ghastly. Color would do no good. The only good would be to leave this place.

Nurses moved swiftly and surely from one patient to the next, and now one came to David to check his vital signs and watch the electrocardiogram trace a diamond-shaped line of his heart motion. I knew a solid black line meant curtains.

Dr. Pigott spoke to reassure, telling me David likely had atrial fibrillation, heartbeat irregularities that must be remedied. Yes, I agreed, yes, do something fast. The doctor told us he was ordering an electric shock treatment to kick David's heart into the proper rhythm, and then, of course, there would be medication.

Electric shock sounded barbaric. "Is there nothing else, Doctor?" I asked. He shook his head, "This is the most effective method to regulate the heart."

David had closed his eyes. I reached again for his hand, cold and limp. He looked like Dad after he'd collapsed on the bathroom floor and the ambulance rushed him to Abbott Hospital in Minneapolis. I still could see Mother huddled beside him as a paramedic strapped the blood pressure cuff to his bony yellowed forearm.

David did share many of Dad's characteristics—the humor, the understanding of the common man and common good, and they both boasted handsome patrician heads with confident broad crowns and chins. It was a "take charge" look, stating, "Stay close to me and all will be well, I will take care of you." But now my father was frail and diminished, and this person on this white bed could not be my lively, funny, handsome husband who awoke joyfully to each day.

Suddenly, just like that, on this sunny, humid July afternoon, thousands of miles away from my family in America, I feared that I was to become a widow. I struggled to hold back tears.

Back in Minnesota, Dad had survived dramatic collapses, but now he required round-the-clock nursing care at home. He was dying in bits and pieces. Mother was never far from his side, always ready to assist the nurse, ready at any moment to bestow her loving care. The journey downhill had been long and painful. All I could think about was the journey they had taken since 1960—twenty-nine years—when a car ran over Mother and him as they crossed a busy street heading for a winter's evening wedding at St. Mark's Cathedral. Perhaps the driver of the car hadn't seen them for they wore dark coats and the sky was black. Dad had realized that the car couldn't stop, and he had pushed Mother to safety and taken the force of the impact. Every bone below his waist was broken, but it was the shock to his nervous system that likely caused the most permanent damage. He was in the hospital for months. He had recovered slowly and regained the strength to realize a retirement ambition. With the assistance of a professional manager, he opened a bookstore in Minneapolis where for ten years he kept regular daily hours until his heart and circulatory system deteriorated.

But after a bathroom fall in 1978, Dad became an invalid. He slept in a hospital bed in a large extra bedroom upstairs, down the hall from Mother and their bedroom. He needed help to eat, to go to the bathroom, and to shower. His nurses insisted on a daily routine. They dressed him and hoisted him into a wheelchair, then to an electric lift hooked to the staircase that carried him to the ground floor. And twice daily Mother and his nurse would prepare him for a ride through the countryside and its rectangles of farms and townships in Mother's red Chevy station wagon. Mother tied a yellow scarf around Dad's neck and placed a visor cap jauntily on his head, brushing his hair from his forehead while his nurse unfolded his gnarled and clenched fists and pushed his stiff arms into a jacket. Then she transferred Dad from his wheelchair to the passenger seat of her red Chevrolet. And my parents began that day's adventure.

During my visits from London I often rode with them, and from the back seat I watched Dad gaze at the fields of barley, soybeans, wheat, corn, and hay, neat, red barns and bungalow houses, Lutheran and Catholic churches, Seven-Eleven stores, bike repair shops, gas stations, VFW halls, and musty corner bars. For each ride Mother chose a different route. She talked to him, but he rarely responded. With a serene expression Dad looked straight ahead. And from the back seat I didn't try to interrupt her; I believe he understood her words, that, as ever, they were communicating perfectly.

From time to time Mother took a break from caregiving. She was a skillful watercolorist, and she joined a class at the local art center to paint once a week. She liked to paint brightly colored spring flowers and winter plants. She framed all her paintings and took great pleasure in hanging them around her house and giving them as presents to her children and grandchildren. And, too, Mother was an active member of the Lake Minnetonka Garden Club. An expert flower arranger, she had earned credentials to judge flower shows around the country. But now she stayed close to home to demonstrate her skills locally for the members of her club. And on many occasions friends would extol to me Mother's talents.

I could hear Mother's friends' words of praise as I stood in the IC Unit looking down at David. Then I heard David making a sound, a low groan, and his eyes opened.

"What's happening?" he asked.

"Darling," I said, leaning in close, "you'll be all right. I can't understand this. You seemed fine this morning."

David had seemed fine that morning. He'd eaten his breakfast, corn flakes and toast, sitting at the center table in the living room. I was just bringing him strong coffee when he called out for a new jar of marmalade, the rough cut stuff. He didn't like runny marmalade and he wanted more butter. That was a routine breakfast, and so was the conversation that accompanied it. And then he had showered and dressed for his semiannual doctor's appointment, but insisted he first give me a ride to the Fulbright office as he said it was too hot for me to take the Underground.

I looked up as Dr. Pigott began to tell me that the electric shock treatment the next day would take only a few seconds, and that David's heart should respond quickly. His voice was matter-of-fact but kind.

I nodded, still trying to grasp the situation. I stared at the several tubes extending from David's body to bags and machines on the wall, the intravenous tube to pour in essential medication, the catheter to empty his bladder. I felt as if I had tumbled into a bizarre nightmare tunnel, and once again, I thought of Mother. She had been attending to Dad for all these years. She seemed selfless, determined, even content. She never complained, simply smiled as she went about her daily routine. But Mother was protected by her heritage and by her status in Minneapolis society. People knew her and respected her. Longtime family retainers surrounded her with care and assistance to maintain the large house and gardens. And family members were close by for support.

I was in a different situation, far away from home in a country where only David appreciated my credentials. To the others I was simply David's wife, the one who had no other task in life but to care for him. I shivered and tightly clasped my arms. Dr. Pigott said goodbye to us both and left the room.

That is when I remembered an incident from years earlier. While downtown at his bookstore, Dad had had a spell, probably a small stroke. Unfortunately Mother was out of town judging a flower show. My brother Ben had collected Dad from the hospital and brought him home, but someone had to stay with him until Mother returned. I had cringed, believing I couldn't possibly give up a day at the Guthrie to care for my father. No, I would hire someone to take my place. When I announced my intention, my sister and brother had looked at me in disbelief. Where was my family loyalty? My sister saved the day when she offered to take a day off of her job at a Wayzata bookstore, but all those years ago I had failed as a caregiver.

I pulled a chair next to David's bed. I could not leave my husband. I would not fail him. I took his hand to stay with him until he fell asleep.

I thought of a childhood memory of my father on that morning in June 1940, the day France had fallen to the Germans. I was seven years old, and on that was the morning I became aware of the War in Europe and the potential danger to all of us.

Each weekday morning at precisely 6:45 my father rose and prepared for the workday. I knew exactly when to join him as he dressed, and I loved these early mornings. That particular morning, as I walked the upstairs hall toward my parents' rooms, I heard Dad's short wave radio crackling and snapping. When I reached their room I saw my father standing in his white boxer shorts and white ribbed singlet, tears running down his cheeks. His head was cocked towards the radio atop his chest of drawers. I heard an English-accented voice speaking rapidly.

"France has fallen," my father said, a catch in his voice. "The Germans have driven their tanks across France and their soldiers have captured Paris."

Seeing my father cry frightened me.

"What will happen now?" I asked. Dad was hunched over on a stool, slowly pulling on his black socks. "It's only time before they cross the English Channel." Dad shook his head.

"Does Mommy know?"

"No, she's still asleep." He looked through the door from their dressing room to an enclosed sleeping porch where they slept in twin beds side by side. Mother always stayed in bed until Dad finished dressing.

I knew about Germany and Hitler; I had seen photographs of this man with a strange black mustache, his hand snapping into a salute before crowds of soldiers and people cheering and saluting. For months every night at dinner Dad had spoken about his fear of Hitler invading Europe and England; he said our President should urge Congress to help these countries. My mother wasn't sure; she didn't want us to go to war.

But now the war was coming close. My parents had English friends; besides, England was just across the Atlantic from New York City, and I had been to New York City. I wondered if the World's Fair I'd attended the previous year was still going on, if people still crowded the boardwalk, laughing and pushing each other, or if the threat of war just across the sea had crushed all the fun of this world.

That morning Dad picked up his silver-backed comb and carefully parted his dark hair. A harsh sandpapery voice continued to issue radio reports, and Dad shook his head as he blew his nose. His nostrils twitched. He selected a blue shirt from a drawer and a gray suit and striped tie from his closet. Fully dressed he sat to run a shoe-buffer over his black shoes before tying the laces. The words from the radio seemed to heighten the importance of each gesture.

I opened the top right bureau drawer to pick out a fresh handkerchief and wondered if today called for a white initialed one or a color. I studied his tie and chose a bright blue-checked hankie to set it off. I handed it to him. "Your favorite," I said, hoping to cheer up my handsome father.

Dad had a fine, sensitive face, a wide smiling mouth and dark brown eyes that crinkled when he laughed, and that was frequently. He told funny, homey stories, jokes on himself and stories about people he saw each day. He was kind and gentle, and when he was relaxing in his armchair, having a drink before dinner, he never seemed to mind my creeping up behind him and ruffling his silky hair. Then I would run to find his comb and "put him back together again," parting his hair as he had just done. His hair smelled of shampoo. Everyday when he took his shower, he shampooed it, which amazed me. I didn't like shampoo. It stung my eyes.

Dad worked downtown at the family wholesale hardware store his grandfather had started before the turn of the century. The store was our family tradition, and that was Dad, a traditionalist. Mother told me people liked him, that he was successful downtown. I didn't know then what success meant, but I guessed it came from being liked. Or maybe I thought success came because Dad dressed in smart clothes and always looked his best, even on weekends in his tan cotton pants and brown checked jacket.

On Dad's bureau with his silver-backed brushes and comb stood two photographs, one a formal one of my mother as a young woman in a black velvet dress. Her hair was naturally wavy, and she was smiling happily. From the texture of that photograph, I could tell she was wearing velvet. The other photograph was the informal snapshot of my parents and me on a September day at the World's Fair, a place and time when the world seemed purely fun.

As Dad finished dressing, I stood and stared at that photograph, willing it to life. Dad moved to stand behind me. "That was a wonderful day," he said. "A wonderful trip just weeks before Hitler..." but he didn't finish. He looked down at the hankie.

"That's just the one I would have picked." He smiled and shook it out and placed it his jacket pocket, all in one motion, like a magician. And much the way the magician's hankie seems the key to magical experience, so my father's blue-checked hankie seemed a vital part of that morning when I awoke to my father's distress at Hitler's advance across Europe and the threat to England.

And now, nearly fifty years later in a hospital on Harley Street looking down at David, his eyes closed, his breathing regular, I thought of all the medical and other crises my father had survived. I prayed David would also. And then, assured that he was peacefully sleeping, I whispered goodnight and walked outside to find our car, to drive home to prepare for tomorrow.

# Remedies for Homesickness

D avid's electric shock treatment failed, but he recovered from this incident and began to understand that he would live longer if he faithfully took the prescribed pills, or tablets as he called them. We enjoyed a slightly shorter summer sailing cruise around some of the islands in the Ionian Sea, and we rejoiced in November when the Russians tore down the Berlin Wall. Within days David and I had made plans with Anne and Peter Thorold to spend a long weekend after New Year's in Berlin to celebrate. Instead I had an emergency hysterectomy after excessive bleeding and scans showed several fibroid tumors. The operation was routine, the tumors benign, but we canceled the trip and I spent those winter months recuperating.

I was no longer working full time. By 1988, our HHHI/U.K. office needed a transfusion of capital. To support our work, we needed new technical equipment, computers and fax machines for which we had no money to purchase. I devised a plan to transfer our operation to the Fulbright Commission to manage as one of its special programs. With Harlan Cleveland and Jim Callaghan's approval, we made the transition and I maneuvered myself out of a job. As a member of the Commission, I still had duties to perform but I could handle most of them at home.

One day that winter of 1990 as I was housebound, David said something like, "Now that you have time, you can scrapbook," and he ordered one of the specially bound books, a large one of a hundred pages. Together we collected from the storeroom boxes of photos and letters and other memorabilia that I had brought from Minnesota, and we sat down at our table to begin the process.

Thinking back, I believe David had another motive in those days. He knew I missed my family, and I'm certain he felt that I should try to turn to positive and tangible reflections. I dreaded those fuzzy, gray edges of homesickness that on occasion crawled into my head, visions of my children and grandchildren going to work and school, the little ones learning to read, play games, make friends, and all this happening without me. I could hear about them through notes and the telephone, but I caught up with their leaps and bounds only at Thanksgiving and Memorial Day weekends. Now that I'd begun to scrapbook, I had a link, pieces of paper that I could arrange to connect me to those I loved and missed.

David galvanized me to action, emphasizing that if I failed now to organize and sort out this material and place it into this book, I would never do it, and all my paper memories would be jumbled and lost. He reminded me once again about thematic placement, mixing photos with clippings and letters, ignoring chronology; themes, he said, were more important, and more interesting to the viewer. So he launched my scrapbooking and then left me alone, only to applaud my efforts at the end of the day.

My first scrapbook began with a photo of Eben and me a week before our marriage, followed by some candid shots of the wedding week. This beginning signaled passage from girlhood to marriage. I left spaces for pertinent material that might turn up later and would add integrity to the page. I combined some of the wedding material with cuttings and photos of my parents' wedding in 1929. On those early pages I pasted bits from our first winter in Orlando where Eben, an F-84 pilot preparing for service in Korea, was stationed for Gunnery school, and then I placed some photos from Fukuoka, Japan, where I had joined him after the Korean war was over.

I pasted a drawing of me with curly black hair and a pearl choker that my son Charlie, aged about eight, had drawn. Next to it, I pasted a recent drawing that, during a Thanksgiving visit to Portland, Charlie's daughter, Megan, almost seven, had drawn of me complete with the same pearl choker. I had received honors both from high school and Smith, so now I pasted some of my school records worthy of note and beside those some of my children's best grades and comments. There was a page for Brothers and Sisters, so I pasted a photo of my mother and her two sisters when they were about thirty, and then several formal photos of me and my siblings taken after my sister was born in 1941. Beside this I placed a photo of Ben, his wife, Joanie, and me that David had taken in Corfu the previous summer. With a pair of sharp scissors and double-sided tape, it was easy. Joyfully inventing my themes and finding the right material to fill the pages, I found the days flew by.

As I sorted, I also made choices, deeming certain items important, others not. I tossed those. I enjoyed the orderly process of taking charge of my life's positive memorabilia. And, there were moments when I wiped away tears, picking up a shot of Eben and me all those years ago holding our boys, or one of the boys and me after our divorce, or postcards the boys had written to me during their late summer visits to their father and stepmother. There were rewarding moments caught on camera—volunteer projects that I had chaired, Tyrone Guthrie in the early '60s on the site of the new theater, and my subsequent work as a volunteer and development director, and best of all the graduation photos of the boys and then the weddings, Chris and Lisa's first on that lovely, misty Marin County February day in 1980, then Charlie and Juli's in 1992 on a crisp June afternoon in Mother's garden bursting with purple pansies, and Michael, the gymnast turned music producer, standing on his head in front of his shelves of CDs in CBS's Los Angeles studio.

I regularly opened the book, sometimes to smile or laugh, caress the page, and often to shed a tear, to wistfully celebrate our combined joys and now the present distance between us. But David

Left: Charlie, Juli, Megan, and Charlie, Jr., Oregon, 1992

Top: Charlie Dobson with Megan,
Chris Dobson with Claire, West Coast, 1987

Below: Chris, Lisa, Claire, Sam, and Pete, California, 1992

Top: Michael, Charlie, and Chris Dobson, 1965

Right: Michael Dobson with Charlie, Jr., Charlie Dobson with Megan, Oregon, 1987

Below: Polly's grandchildren: Megan, Sam, Claire, Pete, and Charlie, Thanksgiving, 1991

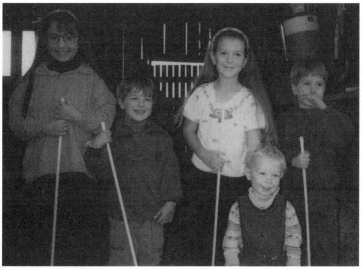

always seemed just around the corner ready to praise a page, to suggest a diversion, to give me a hug. The melancholy would pass. I had too much to celebrate to wallow in sadness.

Over the years David and I often spent winter evenings around our table working on our scrapbooks, talking about the pieces we were assembling. Along with David I clipped cuttings from the British magazines to underscore a theme or to begin a new political page. This was the beginning of years of scrapbooking. After an evening session I moved my book to the top of the chest that sat below our bed. My new scrapbook was always handy to pick up and take to the other room for additions. My inaugural book is huge and heavy, encompassing, finally, the first sixty years of my life. When I moved back to Minnesota, I realized it would be too cumbersome for the fireplace, so I set it on its side in a large drawer of the table next to the sofa and fireplace where I can pull it onto the floor and turn its pages.

Within a few months after I began scrapbooking, I also found another project. As I looked through the boxes of material I found documents of family heritage, references to the heritage of my parents to British sources. My ancestors hailed from the northern counties and Scotland; perhaps, I thought, I ought to find their towns and their graves. At an early age, I had listened to my father describe his English ancestors and their birthplaces. Surely in this material there would be some information to lead me to an ancestral source. I discovered the family tree of my paternal grandmother's ancestors, the Janneys from Cheshire. Thomas Janney was born in Styall, Cheshire, in 1633 and died in Mobberley, Cheshire, in 1697.

My journey to Mobberley would launch an adventure, a search for purpose as much as a desire to find the grave. I was digging for the vein of humor and creativity that ran deep in my father's family. My paternal grandmother, Helen Janney Case, had possessed that vein—my grandmother with her cackling laugh, clad in bright red and blue plaid wool suits, strode purposefully around her domain. She was intelligent, graduating cum laude in

1900 from Smith College. Gangy made up stories, ready quips, never suffered fools gladly, told jokes on herself and her friends. I wanted to trace that humor to its source.

Now I had a project that ignited my imagination. Would I discover the characteristics I so loved in my father—his gentleness, wit, and intelligence? Could I trace these qualities back to their source? And what, then, would I know about myself—would I discover the source of a certain sensitivity, a desire for risk and adventure?

On a day's trip to Mobberley I was disappointed not to discover my ancestor's grave in the Anglican graveyard. During a subsequent trip to the County seat in Chester, I found that Thomas Janney had been a Quaker. I knew nothing about the Quakers and their religious practice. Here then was research for a new project.

Back in London as I sharpened my pencil at the Quaker librarian's desk (I took notes with pencils to prevent ink blot damage to the fragile aging texts), I felt inspired. In a flash I had rediscovered the magic of my working years, and I knew I would now thoroughly research and annotate and write a book, one I would dedicate to my grandchildren. This would be my gift to them— the detailed revelations of their heritage.

For the next several years I tried to spend several mornings or afternoons a week at the Quaker Library. Often I ate a simple lunch in the cafeteria or took a sandwich to a bench in the inner courtyard. At the center of the courtyard, water flowed through an iron fountain and pots of leafy ficus plants and bright marigolds and asters enclosed this quiet place. Sitting there I always felt a sense of the Quaker peace enfolding me in its embrace, a sense of wellbeing, of being in the right place, alone but not lonely. Here in this place was light, a sense of inner worth and affirmation.

One day in the archives, I held in my hands Thomas Janney's original letters, letters he wrote from Pennsylvania at the end of the 17th century as well as letters sent to English Friends. Quaker historians, I discovered, had written books about the Janneys, their early settlements in Pennsylvania and Virginia and their leadership within Quaker communities. A distantly related uncle, Samuel

Janney, a 19th-century scholar and historian, had published a quartet of books detailing the early history of the Society of Friends.

Each evening over dinner David would ask about my day's progress. I knew he would be especially happy when I began to write the story, as I would then work at home. He liked me close by.

As I moved from the 17th to the 18th and 19th centuries, I relished the letters exchanged between my great-grandfather Phineas and his son, Thomas Benton. I could discern a light-hearted character, a man who did not take himself too seriously. These men were merchants and hardware dealers. Here were the roots of my father's Minneapolis business.

The more I learned, the more I mused about my father's compassion, about his kindness and belief that each human being harbors a kernel of goodness, of intelligence. He believed that each person had a gift, a God-given talent. Although Dad was a devout Episcopalian, at heart, I now understood, he was a Quaker. He was good and generous, industrious and thoughtful to a fault. He hated war, had never borne arms, never shot a bird or animal. He was too young to serve in the first World War and too old for the second. I did often wonder if he hadn't been too old if he would have enlisted and requested a staff job.

My father never told a malicious story about anyone else, though he often joked self-deprecatingly about himself. He read voraciously, as if making up for leaving college before graduation. As he put it, he'd done the four-year course in three at Princeton, though in truth he left Princeton after freshman year, before the university asked him not to return. He had neglected his studies for a lively social life. After that first year at Princeton, he joined Janney, Semple, Hill, the family wholesale hardware.

After months of research, with my father's family tales churning in my head and heart, I was ready to write the story. I bought a laptop computer and each day set it up on the center table in the sitting room in our tiny flat. I trailed various cords to electrical outlets around the room and tiny foyer, and each evening I dismantled the arrangement to set the table for dinner. On those days David and I ate lunch at home, I dismantled the equipment twice a day.

In May the following year we moved to a larger flat across the street in Cranmer Court and there I converted a small second bedroom into my office. Now I had my "Room of One's Own." Each day I continued the routine I had established at the library, though twice a week I took a break from scholarship to play tennis with girlfriends, and on weekends David and I sailed on our small sloop moored on the Beaulieu River near Southampton.

Still, each afternoon after lunch I would sit in my hideaway and write until 7 P.M. David swam each afternoon at the Berkeley Hotel swimming pool and afterwards he called on elderly friends, so I always could count on at least four hours of solitude. Whenever I needed to resolve some tangle in my writing, I would leave the flat and take a short walk around the Green or through St. Luke's churchyard. Inspiration always arrived. Walks were my constructive solace, my source of new thoughts and confidence. I put together an outline and resolved to complete the book in two years. I would not deviate from my schedule; that would be a betrayal not only of myself but of my grandchildren.

Now I learned that for several hundred years, the Janneys had been traders, owning and operating export/import businesses; they'd been storekeepers, hardware men. Brief notes in the books in the London library now became full and rich with detail. My family pursuits had kept a steady course over the centuries.

David and I visited Philadelphia and Virginia to meet some of my "extended family." A Smith classmate and her husband hosted us in northern Virginia where we met a venerable cousin, Asa Moore Janney, in his late eighties and still commanding a desk at the family store in Goose Creek. As I listened to Asa Moore reel off tales, I felt bound to my distant cousin by sympathetic humor and common values. I suddenly understood that beneath my grandmother's often acerbic humor welled a deep feeling for those less fortunate than she, and again my father's qualities came to mind. I shouted my joy to a smiling but quite deaf Asa Moore.

When I was finished I sat in my "Room of One's Own" and looked around, full, joyful. I had written a book, albeit a small one, eighty-eight pages, set off by a stunning cover designed by the resident artist at Sessions. Thomas Janney, "Publisher of Truth," sits astride his horse as he embarks on his journeys. The drawing was more than a cover design to me; it was a symbol, a signal of my continuing journey. I had more family stories to tell, more adventures of the family pioneers as they organized new communities, moving from Pennsylvania, to Virginia, to Illinois, and finally Minnesota.

This was my first book. I had already begun to research the second, a story of an 18th-century family matriarch, Hannah, who was born in Philadelphia, and moved with her husband and children to Loudoun County, Virginia, before the Revolutionary War. I set part of the story against the backdrop of the war. Hannah was a Quaker minister. And then the third book, the 19th-century tale of Phineas and his family, who traveled from Virginia across the Ohio river to the midwest and eventually to Minneapolis in 1875. The Civil War formed the background for this story, which concluded with my grandmother's matriculation at Smith College. On the day of my birth, Gangy had enrolled me in Smith, and I had come full circle, nurtured and filled by an Inner Light. And I had begun a writing career.

# Mother

Here now, all these years later, in my tiny den, my writing space, the Quaker books stand on a shelf near the window, but, as I look around this space, I find my mother. She rests at the back of the couch within her intricately designed needlepoint pillows and on the walls behind her watercolor paintings of the flowers she loved—daffodils, tulips, azaleas, hyacinths, and lilies—and there she is on my desk in the framed black and white photograph of her and my father, circa 1965.

In this photograph Mother, cheekbones distinctly defined, is smiling happily at the photographer. She wears a fashionable cocktail dress as she sits next to Dad at a New York City restaurant table. She is about sixty years old. Her elbows rest on the table with her hands clasped together.

Mother's nails were always lovely, like unbroken sea shells. Regularly a manicurist shaped each one, pushed back the cuticles and filed the nail to a uniform length just over the finger tip; over this she applied a light coat of clear polish. And Mother was careful about her lovely hands. She never gestured or made a fist. Her hands usually rested quietly on a table or her lap or nimbly worked her knitting needles, each groomed finger engaged in its own important role, unraveling a skein, holding a strand of wool, or moving the needles. Through the years Mother knitted baby sweaters and booties for her children and grandchildren, and she created complicated, patterned argyle socks for all her close male relatives. Her needles were never still. They seemed to move unconsciously under her control as she focused her full attention on my father, as they sat together in the library with their pre-dinner martinis.

With her discerning eyes and clever fingers, Mother also mastered watercolor painting. She was fond of telling us children how tricky this was; the painter, she explained, could stroke the brush just once across the paper and must make no mistake nor try to do it over. Oils, she claimed, were much easier. And so Mother painted watercolors.

Her hands, like her voice, were never raised in anger or exhilaration. That, I'm afraid, has not always been my pattern.

My mother enjoyed ninety-three years of life. From early childhood I was aware of her courage. She bravely accepted seven months of bed rest in order to carry her babies—my three siblings—to full term, sacrificing her vigorous life to ensure a healthy family.

I will always remember that May evening in 1941. I was eight years old. As usual Dad was playing his radio while he and Mother enjoyed their pre-dinner drinks. He played the radio all the time, before breakfast, and after he came home from the office, and all weekend. On and on, he listened to the war reports of Hitler's control of Western Europe and relentless bombing of England. I thought maybe that was why Dad was frowning so much. He hadn't gotten into the Army. They didn't want him. He told us that was because he was too old, and because his back hurt.

But a few minutes later at the dinner table we shifted to news of our home. Mother announced she would be going to bed the next day and would remain there for seven months until the birth of my new brother or sister. This was terrible news.

Mother was so energetic, so full of life and sparkle. I shuddered to think of her in bed throughout my summer vacation, into the new school year, all the way to Christmas. I swallowed hard and struggled to hold back my tears.

Polly's childhood home, Wayzata, Minnesota, circa 1940

"Time will go fast, Polly," she tried to reassure me. "We'll read books and you'll pick out my nighties and bed jackets." That didn't help.

How had this happened? I didn't know how babies got started but I figured it had to have something to do with Mother and Dad and I hadn't seen them hugging or kissing. They slept in twin beds. Sometimes when I walked into their bedroom, I found them snuggled in one bed, together. Still, I couldn't imagine how a bit of snuggling could make a baby and send Mother to bed for seven months. That seemed forever.

That evening, as she tucked me into bed, she leaned close to explain the problem. She would lose the baby if she got out of bed. She used the word "miscarriage." She explained that a mother must hold her baby inside her for nine months for the baby to be healthy and strong, and she reminded me that she had stayed in bed with my younger brothers, Ben and Charlie. I remembered her bedridden with Charlie only three years earlier. She went on to say that she'd been lucky with me, that I had survived a premature birth, but she could take no chances. I didn't understand, but before I could cry, Mother kissed my cheek, stood, and began to walk out of my room. I looked at her, so slim, her gray flannel skirt fitting snugly over narrow hips. At the door, she turned and smiled and gave me a wave.

The sun was setting. It was a warm evening. I lay on my back looking at the ceiling. Summer was almost here. Tears trickled down the back of my throat. I rubbed my hand over my tummy, and pulled up the top of my new pink flowered summer pajamas, using the soft corner to wipe my eyes.

Mother's confinement developed a definite pattern. During those summer months, she remained at the heart of the household bustle, her hospital bed set up on the downstairs screened porch overlooking her garden and its lush perennials. Faithfully, at least twice a day during my school holidays, Ben and I climbed up onto Mother's bed, curled up on each side of her to listen to her read *Grimm's Fairy Tales*, *Little House on the Prairie*, and *Black Beauty* until her voice grew hoarse. A nurse lived in the house to care for her. She hooked rugs, knitted baby clothes for the baby-to-be and socks for Dad, and she smilingly received visitors, close family and friends, and several times a day my little brother, Charlie, would toddle to her bedside and the nurse would lift him to her lap for a hug.

Dad spent more time with me than he had in the past. On Saturday mornings, he took me to his office in a different section of Minneapolis, far from my grandparents' houses, my school, and St. Mark's Cathedral. Dad's hardware store and warehouse were close to the Mississippi River, one block from the Great Northern railroad station. He parked his car on the far side of the station, explaining to me that he liked to walk by Molly's newsstand on his way to the office. I could smell the soot from the trains, and I was careful to step over large black cracks that veined the sidewalks. We waited for a streetcar to pass before we crossed to Molly's stand.

"Hello there, Ben," Molly called out to Dad.

"Hello, Mol, how are you getting along?"

"Okay, slow on Saturdays, you know."

"Well, then I'll just buy a *Chicago Tribune*." Dad fished in his pocket for some change.

"This your little girl, Ben?"

"This is Polly."

I offered my hand, and Molly smiled at me through a few teeth, teeth as black as the cracks in those sidewalks. Her hair was matted and a funny, rusty color, like iced tea. But I knew I should like her, Dad did. We said goodbye and walked on, heading towards his office. I looked around at the quiet street, at a few old men sitting on a bench sorting clothes from a burlap sack.

Dad said, "Let's go look at the river before we go to the office." So we turned back towards the Hennepin Avenue Bridge, and when we reached it we stood at the edge, looking down at the water thundering towards St. Anthony Falls. Dad told me that Molly was a person who lived on the streets; these people had no homes, he explained, and sometimes no family. She had lost track of her children long ago. His voice had that funny quiver in it that it sometimes had.

"What about her husband?" I asked.

"Oh, he disappeared before her children did," Dad said.

I let this new information wash over me the way the water washed over the rocks below. No kids, no husband, no home, I couldn't imagine. How sad and lonely that must be. And no place for shelter. I couldn't imagine how anyone could stay outside all year long. Winters. I looked at my dad. "What about winter?" I asked.

Dad smiled at me, and then he began to walk towards the office. As we walked he talked about special places where homeless people stayed. Shelters, he called them, but they weren't guaranteed. He told me about the welfare programs, but, he added, they never covered every need. Homeless people were hungry and depressed, he said, and Molly was fortunate even to have newspapers to sell. Perhaps one day she would have permanent shelter, an apartment, and she could "better her predicament," he said, though I thought he looked sad when he said that. He said she was a determined woman and he wanted to help her, help her keep her job.

"It gives her dignity," he said, which was a word I didn't know; but once he said it, I thought I understood. "When a person is down and out," he went on, "that person doesn't have dignity. People scorn that person, and then he is hopeless."

Dad unlocked the front door of the large brick building that housed the hardware store, and we walked up a few wooden steps to another door with a glass window. When we pushed open the door we entered a large room arranged in cubicles separated by glass and wood, each one with a desk and chair. On each desk an enormous typewriter stood, and from the ceiling metal tubes swung down. Dad explained the tubes were for sending messages back and forth between the floors. Dad's office was a larger cubicle, but he had no typewriter, only a large desk and armchair on wheels and bookcases filled with catalogs. He instructed me to sit at his secretary's empty desk and use her colored pencils while he read some letters and dictated responses into a large metal horn attached to a machine like a small record player. On Monday, his secretary would play back the recordings, he said. Then she would type the letters. That's why he had no typewriter.

I doodled with a few pencils and thought about Molly. Her world seemed so far from my sheltered one. I often played under the willow tree in the backyard, hiding under its long yellowy green branches, reading books and making up imaginary people and stories. But the moment the air turned cold or rain started to fall, I simply dashed inside, into our warm kitchen, where I was treated to the pleasures of cookies and milk. And to the warmth of our family.

I drew pictures of the willow tree and our play yard and me on my bicycle, and before I'd finished Dad turned off his machine and took my hand. It was time to go home.

During the summer that Mother lay in bed, her mother, my Grandmother Cobby, invited me to join her and my grandfather for several weeks at Beaver Bay.

On the north shore of Minnesota, stretching into Lake Superior's icy waters, is a peninsula shaped like a beaver's body and marked with birch trees, Norway pines, and log cabins. The original settlers called it Beaver Bay. During the 1920s Minneapolis friends built most of the thirteen cabins as a means to escape the city's humid heat. Sitting where the "beaver" body joins the mainland, the town of Beaver Bay, a community of several cafes, bars, a gas station, post office, and agate shop, awaits its summer customers.

During the five-hour car ride I noticed gray granite and rusty iron-colored rocks, steep cliffs rising or falling from the road, resorts scattered along the highway offering wooden cottages for rent, some with outhouses in back. Finally we arrived at our destination, making a right turn at Lorntsen's cafe to a red gravel road, log cabins on each side and in the middle of the property a lodge where a local cook and several helpers prepared and served all our meals. Both sets of my grandparents owned cabins here. Mother's parents had built a roomy cabin at the end of the peninsula with a plate glass window overlooking the bay.

At Beaver Bay I roamed through groves of white birch and Norway pines. I crept under pine branches sweeping the ground, a sheltering willow and its dark green needled carpets, my favorite hiding place. I walked over spongy ground decorated by tiny wildflowers that crept out between the stones and rocks. There were tiny white bunch berries and field flowers, goldenrod which made my eyes itch and nose run. Cobby said that I had inherited my father's hay fever. I didn't care, I loved the colors and names like Pink Fireweed, orange Indian Paintbrush, and Black-eyed Susan. Why couldn't I be called Susan? If Mother's baby was a girl, maybe she would be Susan.

As autumn approached Mother and her apparatus moved upstairs to my parents' sleeping porch. She was able to rest more now that we were in school, but by four o'clock Ben and I were back home, and I would rush upstairs. Passing through my parents' dressing room, I sometimes stopped at her dotted-Swiss cotton dressing table, sat in the chair with its waffle-woven cane seat and stared into space. This was where Mother used to sit, before she was getting babies and confined to bed. Here she had dressed for dinner parties, often in a raspberry-red velvet party dress, and here she would run a comb through her wavy hair, spray her Chanel Number 5, then slip her tongue over her lips coated in bright red lipstick. I always laughed when she stood up because her bottom would be stamped with a waffle pattern.

Now I couldn't resist opening her dressing-table drawers. There were treasures there—her small chamois cloth jewelry boxes, beaded evening bags, a stack of white gloves, monogrammed hankies amidst lavender and gardenia scented sachets, and bobby pins and extra ribbons for my pigtails, and those pink plaster patches that she wore to relax her forehead frowns. A silver dish brimmed with pins and cough drops. The dish had been a trophy for winning a mixed doubles tennis tournament at the country club. Not with Dad—he had a bad back—but with a friend of theirs who Mother said was athletic. When would she wear that sharkskin tennis dress and perky white cap again? When would she dress in that soft velvet dress and pick a beaded bag to match?

I closed the drawers and walked towards the porch. Her tummy was becoming rounder and harder every day. Was this what having babies was all about? If so, I didn't want them. If it happened to Mother, it would surely happen to me. And I didn't like the thought one bit.

"Pol, is that you?" Mother called out, clearly.

"Here I am. Guess what we're doing at school?" All day long I'd been aching to tell her my story. Over the past year I had learned a lot about the war, about England particularly and the nightly German bombing. There was a program called Bundles for Britain, a collection of packages of clothing and goods for English people who were suffering so much. At Brownie meetings and during our fourth grade class, we talked about projects that would help to raise money, and I'd had the idea to do a play, *Red Riding Hood*, our class production for the entire school; everyone would pay a dime to attend and we would send our proceeds to England.

I told Mother that I would play the lead role, choose my friends to play the other parts, and direct the production, and that Miss Spurr, the school principal, had approved the benefit.

"Pol, that's wonderful," Mother said. "You thought of it all by yourself. Good for you."

"But I'll miss you there, Mummy," I paused, thinking maybe Essie could come. Essie was our nurse, not really for me or Ben, but for our younger brother, Charlie, and for Mother's new baby.

For all those months, we coasted peacefully along, mindful of Mother's condition. I was busy with schoolwork and *Red Riding Hood*. Ben and I tried to play quietly and stop teasing each other before a grownup scolded us. We knew Mother would be normal again one of these days. At least that's what everyone said.

Each evening when Dad returned from the office, he gently kissed my mother, then strode to the pantry to collect the things he needed to mix their martinis. On a large wooden tray he placed two specially-shaped glasses with stems, a bottle of gin and vermouth, a large silver shaker and a small ice bucket filled from trays in the kitchen icebox. Then he emptied ice cubes into the shaker. He never measured gin, just poured it straight into the shaker and then added a tiny drop of vermouth. "That's all you need of this French stuff," he said. "Any more than a drop ruins the drink. It has to be very dry."

Each evening I listened as Dad offered Mother news from Minneapolis, bits of gossip and business talk he had gathered at his Minneapolis Club lunches, and they talked easily with each other.

"Oh, Darling," she would say, "how funny, that sounds just like Bill," and Dad would echo her laugh and refill her glass. When it was time for dinner, she ate from a tray placed on a hospital table that rolled across her bed, and Dad sat at her bedside, eating from a tray. Dinners in the dining room had been suspended, and I was back in the kitchen for an early dinner with my brothers. Essie ate with us and asked us about school, gently admonishing us not to talk with our mouths full and to use our knives to cut the meat, not saw it with a fork.

I liked to watch Edith, our cook, prepare our meals, especially the evenings she prepared Mother's favorite, vanilla ice cream with hot caramel sauce. At the stove Edith would whip a tin spoon round the saucepan to keep the melting sugar from scorching, and as we sat at the table finishing our shepherd's pie and peas, we sniffed that sweet toffee aroma. She was an expert. She poured in a bit of cream at just the right moment, creating the creamiest sauce imaginable.

"Can I take the spoon to Mother to lick?" I would always ask, and Edith always told me I had to finish eating first, must let Mother and Dad have their cocktails.

But I would beg. I wanted to see Mother laugh and smack her lips as she pulled the tin spoon through her teeth. And, of course, I wanted to be a part of their conversation. So I wore Edith down. She would pour the sauce into a pitcher, hand me the saucepan and spoon, and, careful of my prize, I'd climb the stairs to their porch. When Mother saw me, she set down her martini glass.

"Oh, Pol, how did you know I wanted to lick the pan?," and then Mother lifted the spoon to her mouth in a looping gesture while Dad went on talking—about the Farmers Mechanics Bank board meeting or the prospects of a winning football season for the Golden Gophers.

Many nights I stayed over at my best friend, Harriett's, house. Her parents were outwardly affectionate with each other and their children. They frequently kissed each other on the lips and said, "I love you." "Love you, too," would come the swift reply, even at the breakfast table where Harriett's mother fed whole wheat bread into a toaster on the dining room table and buttered each piece as it popped out. I asked my mother why we couldn't have a toaster on our table at breakfast and brown bread instead of Wonder bread. But Mother was still in her bed awaiting her baby, far from the breakfast table, and she brushed away my question. I thought about leaning over and kissing her, telling her I loved her. I wanted that hot buttery toast and those kisses, but we kissed only on the cheeks in our house. I knew Mother loved me, but no one spoke these words aloud. My parents never did.

By December Mother's tummy was as big as a watermelon and just as hard. She told me everything inside her would stretch and the baby would come right out, but I still imagined my baby brother or sister simply dropping out onto the floor, and I worried about that.

Then one Sunday morning, I woke to find the snow dusty-gray in the early dawn darkness. I tiptoed to their sleeping porch where Mother was talking softly to my father. Her feet dangled over the edge of the bed as she struggled to stand. At last. This was the week she would have her baby—the hole would stretch and out the baby would pop and by Christmas Mother would be her old self, with a new baby in the nursery. I hoped for a sister.

Dad helped Mother to sit, placing a hand behind her back and moving her legs to the side of the bed, but he seemed worried; the radio was turned on.

"Here I am, can I help?" I called from the doorway.

My parents smiled. "I'll get your robe," I said. "I love the peach one. It's so velvety and it smells like you, Mommy, like gardenias."

"The peach one is perfect," Mother said. She had not worn a bathrobe for seven months. I helped her place the robe around her shoulders and then she called out to Dad.

"Oh, that radio, I'm so tired of it all. I want to get up. Ben, help me!"

But for the first time my father didn't call sweetly to her.

"Quiet," he shouted as he announced the terrible news that the Japanese had bombed Pearl Harbor. The harbor was burning and many ships had been sunk. He moved to my mother's side, placing an arm around her shoulder.

I didn't know what to do. I could see my mother trying to stand, adjusting her robe, and my father in front of the radio. I was terrified. It seemed the entire world was upside down. I stood still and trembled.

My mother stretched out her hands and he slowly pulled her to her feet. She swayed forward, her stomach so large it pulled her forward. She paused to regain her balance, took Dad's arm and tottered slowly, her first steps in seven months. She sat down in a stuffed arm chair and smiled. But Dad looked like he was going to cry. His voice shook as he continued to talk about this horrible surprise attack by the Japanese. As I looked at their worried faces, I was afraid. I can't remember how we spent the next hours.

At the end of that grim day, at cocktail time, my father did seem happier. He mixed their drinks and we sat on the porch and listened to the news. I perched on the floor at their feet. Mother, still wrapped in her peach velvet robe, sat in an armchair sipping her martini, intently listening to the news reports, and occasionally her eyes found Dad's. Ben walked into the room and sat down next to me. Somehow I knew that everywhere around the world families were huddled close to their radios, listening. We all leaned in.

"War is all over the world," I explained to Ben. "Do you know about the Japanese?" He was listening too. I grabbed his hand. I wanted us all to be safe, and I wanted the new baby, and I wanted that new baby to be the sister, Carolyn, who did arrive four days later on December 11. We called her CC after Mother's sister. I was so happy to have a little doll that I could hold and help to bathe and dress, happy too that Mother was back with us again, standing and moving about the house, hugging us, walking up the stairs and helping us to bed. She was slowly recovering her figure. After months in bed, she was weak, yet heavy all over. Her face was like a pumpkin. Every day, she exercised with a woman who came to massage and help strengthen her muscles.

So with all that joy in the house I tried not to think about the war, but the radio and newspapers provided all the frightening information about the Japanese defeating the American troops on those tiny Pacific islands. At mealtimes my parents discussed the war, though joy and laughter soon prevailed since they doted on my sister and their three other healthy children. Mother's demanding pregnancies were behind her. The future seemed bright.

Over the years I have wondered if I possess Mother's fortitude. I was never tested in the way she was. Spontaneously Eben and I conceived Charlie a year after our marriage. I never doubted that I could become pregnant nor that I would continue to lead an active life as I carried the babies to full term. My pregnancies were joyous, and I gave birth naturally after about four hours of labor. Mother had not prepared me for labor pains. "Nothing," she had said, "Nothing. Just a few pangs and then a push." Well, it wasn't that way, but that was Mother's stoic attitude. Charlie was born in 1954, after Eben and I returned from the Far East, and his tour of duty in the Air Force. Chris was born in 1956 when we were living in Nevada, Iowa, near Des Moines, while Eben learned the family lumber business, and Michael was born in 1958 in Minneapolis.

Mother had set an example and I observed her carefully. Throughout her life Mother planned each day with precision, and at the end of their lives, my parents continued to be an impregnable union. When I close my eyes I see my mother preparing my father for a twice-daily car ride, releasing first his fists, then smoothing his hair, and tilting his cap. Mother lived for nine years after my father's death. But during the last twelve years of his life as an invalid, she was saying goodbye to him quietly and stoically. Occasionally she shed a private tear, ones that we would only see if we entered her bedroom to find her standing by the window overlooking her garden.

Not long ago, on Mother's Day, my daughter-in-law, Juli, asked if I had saved any of Mother's clothes. I said my sister had given some to her grandchildren but we had given away or we had lost many of her beautiful stylish dresses. They lived in my memory. So I wrote this poem.

## My mother, Polly

*You gave me your name,*
*your love of family and life and boundless energy.*
*I see you sliding down the Beaver River Falls in your funny old-fashioned*
*faded blue checked bathing suit with the pleated skirt,*
*showing us ten-year-olds how to slip into the main stream, onward to the falls,*
*laughing lustily as your tiny bottom hit the sharp rock points*
*hiding under root-beer colored water.*
*Brave you were then and brave always.*
*Juli asks about your lovely dresses, satins and silks,*
*hanging all those years in plastic bags in the cedar closet.*
*They are memories now; we let them go,*
*without regret, as smoothly as you slid so slippery in the foaming waters*
*on a blistering hot August afternoon...*

Even now that my mother is gone, I feel her nurturing spirit. I can almost hear her asking me to remember, explore, and celebrate the loves, losses, and recoveries of my life.

Often during my growing-up years, Mother told me that men enjoyed talking to her because she was a good listener. She told me they liked to dance with her because she rested her hand like a feather on their shoulders and because she was light on her feet. She said that was the way to do it.

But what Mother didn't tell me, perhaps because she didn't know, was how to make male friendships. It was one thing to be light on your feet and twirl around the dance floor, flirting slightly with a shift of one's eyes, and yet quite another to develop and master friendships. It took many years for me to discover openness and trust and the confidence to speak honestly. Without knowing it, this was what I was learning. As the years passed David and I became not only husband and wife but beloved friends.

# Bellatrix

David named our new boat *Bellatrix* for the navigational star. She was a beauty, a sloop rigged thirty-four-foot fiberglas boat built a year after I arrived in London, at the Westerly boat yard near Winchester. Almost from the first time David and I met, he had talked of his retirement dream, a boat to cruise the warm waters of the Mediterranean and the Ionian Seas, a boat that, as time permitted, we could join and rejoin. Her winter port would be wherever we finished our summer cruise, and during the rest of the year we would still sail on the Solent in his wooden smack, *Sall*. I heartily endorsed his dream, and during one of my earliest visits to David we toured various boatyards and the boat shows to find the right model for us. The Westerly yard produced the most efficient and serviceable boat for us.

*Bellatrix* was comfortably rigged and designed below, with an owners' quarters in the stern, then the galley and saloon with benches around the center table that could slide out for bunks, and forward quarters with another head, or bathroom. She was a fine accommodation for us and for the crew, friends and family, who from time to time joined us.

David arranged for the boat to be transported across the Channel to France and to Cogolin, a port near St. Tropez on the south coast. That first summer we planned to spend six weeks, mid-July through August, sailing her westward along the French coast, down the coast of Spain to Majorca, where David's eldest daughter and her family were holidaying. As August is a traditional European holiday month, I easily negotiated the time away from my job.

We left London, driving our car, to the channel port of Dover to board the car ferry for the seventy-five minute ride to Calais. We sat outside on the ferry's top deck where the sea air was contagious, the gulls overhead flapping and screeching a boisterous holiday greeting. At Calais we drove the car onto a train transport and boarded our own compartment-cabin. There we languished in splendor with wine and a picnic supper as the train began its journey to Nice.

Next morning I opened the window curtains to behold the architecture of the south of France blazing with Mediterranean browns, peaches, golds, and pinks. At Nice we collected a dirty car and drove along the Cote d'Azur to Cogolin. I noticed the unusual vegetation, tall Australian pines, dry soil, rocky coast, warm air, and the dazzling sun that year after year draws so many Brits to this coast.

We boarded *Bellatrix*, spent several days provisioning and checking equipment, and then, joined by friends, we set sail for the several days' passage to Majorca. At Porto Pollenca we berthed at a yacht club and sailed by day with members of David's family, anchoring in a variety of small coves along the shore for swimming and snorkeling. At the end of August we secured *Bellatrix* at a marina for the winter and flew to France and our car for the drive back to London.

Nine months later, in late May, David and a crew traveled to *Bellatrix* to sail her to Corsica. He returned to London in June and we both joined her in mid-July to sail around Corsica, to Elba, and to the Tuscan coast of Italy. One morning while still in Corsica I walked from a shop to see David at a small outdoor restaurant table sipping white wine and eating half a lobster. He asked me to take his photograph to tease his sister, Molly, who fussed about his "devil-may-care" diet. I had given up coaxing him to eat more vegetables and fruits, less cream and fewer carbohydrates. Over the years his weight had fluctuated up and down depending on whether he was paying attention to his doctor, who had been urging him for years to lose pounds, to reduce the threat of high cholesterol and heart problems. He seemed to understand these warnings, but as he never retained any information about food values and calories, he would drink and eat as and when he pleased. I studiously avoided food confrontations as the results were nonproductive. He was not changing his habits or his cravings for sweets.

We ate most meals aboard, where I did have some control. I planned a dinner routine: pasta one night, risotto the second, omelets the third. We enjoyed drinks in *Bellatrix*'s cockpit while the water boiled for the pasta, and then we ate below in the saloon if the evening was cool. On warm nights we carried our plates up on deck. But after three or four nights it was time for a welcome fish dinner ashore. Eating outside on the various wharfs was always a treat except for the hundreds of cats patrolling the tables, scrounging food. As a non-cat person I resented the furry bodies pawing at my bare legs as I lifted a delicious morsel of calamari to my mouth. I loved the Mediterranean squid. In fact I ordered it almost every night, lightly fried or grilled in its own ink, a far cry from Lake Minnetonka perch. David topped off each meal ashore with a Mediterranean ice cream delicacy, a "Tartuffe," a ball of vanilla or chocolate ice cream covered with a chocolate coating, much like the American Cheerios. These were served on a plate and eaten with fork and spoon.

But being by ourselves on *Bellatrix* was best, for there we had our privacy and quiet time, no fussing about requests for special jams and teas we didn't have on board or having to converse throughout the day. At port we relaxed in the afternoon and read or walked ashore when we felt like it, examining the produce and handcrafted goods in the marketplaces and traversing the tiny streets that crisscrossed neighborhoods beyond the harbor. Village life here in these Mediterranean countries offered a restful contrast to a fast-paced London life.

As we followed Napoleon's footsteps, we discovered these islands contained a wealth of history. After we made fast at a harbor quay, I took off to prowl the streets searching for the houses with the plaques noting the historical occupants. From Corsica we sailed to Portoferio, the major port of Elba. There on the hill above the harbor, I found the house where Napoleon lived after Waterloo and before his incarceration on St. Helen's, and took David back the next day. History at my footsteps.

We berthed in the old commercial harbor, although we sailed every day in surrounding waters, anchoring for lunch and swimming. I loved diving off the bow into unknown waters, the water cold and the tide pulling. I had to swim quickly back to the ladder. Often the force of the tide lifted the top of my bikini off my shoulders, but no one minded. This was the Med, where anything goes.

David was the skipper, in charge of all operations. We did, of course, go over the day-by-day tasks ashore, and one of mine was filling the ice chest. I would travel by bus ride to the ice house, a small wooden building about ten minutes away in the middle of Portoferio. There I grasped the large chunks of ice and heaved them into canvas sail bags, paid the owner who sat smoking in a little cubicle, then reboarded the bus. As the ice began to melt on my legs, I'd wonder if I would make it to the boat before too much dripped away.

Our favorite restaurant in Portoferio was Dante's, located right on the harbor. Bene, the proprietor, clad in large white tennis shoes and black shorts darted from table to table taking and filling orders himself. We loved his pasta, and of course, his calamari, and David always spoke in Italian to Bene, complimenting the food and engaging in a conversation. David said he spoke like a Neapolitan taxi driver. Whatever he thought, I marveled at his competence with this beautiful language. I communicated only with nouns and sign language.

The Italian ports and marinas required a stern-to position for docking the boats. To me this was an intricate maneuver. First

I dropped the anchor forward to steady the boat, then David, his back to the quay, reversed gear to move into the designated spot. I leapt quickly from bow to stern, grabbing lines, ready to jump ashore. David was so skilled and practiced that this procedure usually went off without a hitch, but I was always nervous, reacting to the commotion, the shouting and movements of other sailors on the quay. David explained that Italian sailors always shout and gesture with their arms and fists, that it meant nothing, just hearty good will, their way of communicating. This wasn't the same expression of good will that I remembered sailing at the Lake Minnetonka Yacht Club or along the gulf coast of Tampa Bay.

Still, I learned to like our docking routines, tossing the lines in a straight trajectory to the quay. Sometimes a sailor from another boat was there to take them, or, when no one was, I I jumped ashore to grab and secure the lines around bollards or through metal rings. Each season I had to relearn the Bowline knot, and at first I was all thumbs, but after practice I could twist it in seconds. I also learned to respond well to the helpful Italian shouting. I ignored the rising decibels and tried to understand the language and gradually relaxed in the south Med atmosphere.

Our destination during that summer of 1987 was Porto Ercole, along the coast of Tuscany. There we docked at the town quay for several weeks and welcomed friends who arrived in successive batches to crew. During this second summer of *Bellatrix* I was learning to relax, savoring the Med and the towns and the hospitality we provided. The days were filled with sun and water and David's lighthearted humor and natural grace with our guests. While sailing he often gave each guest a turn at the helm, taught novices about the ways of boating, and created a warm and expansive atmosphere on *Bellatrix* which I found contagious. I looked at him remembering my father's gentle manner as he taught us children basic rules of boating and water safety while he maneuvered his small Chris Craft motorboat around the bays of Lake Minnetonka.

Thinking back to my years sailing with Ted Brown on the gulf coast, I remembered Ted's reluctance to spend time reassuring novice sailors or sharing control of the helm. There was no such problem with *Bellatrix*'s knowledgeable and gracious skipper, and I basked in this generous spirit.

To be feared was the Meltami, a fierce wind from the north coast of Africa. One day, we sailed with five friends to a picnic on a tiny island off Port Ercole. After lunch as we set sail, we noted the distinct line of a weather front to our west. Almost before we knew it, wind and rain hit. David ordered the others below, and as the temperature dropped, he asked me to give him his favorite Canadian lumber jacket. He stood, with great strength, at the helm holding *Bellatrix* into the wind. We could see nothing anywhere near, absolutely alone in a tempest.

"It won't last long," David called to comfort the others, who were anxiously peering from the companion way. I was terrified also but tried to concentrate on him and what he was trying to do. I felt more secure near him so I refused to leave his side, giving him what support I could muster, sitting on the floor of the cockpit beneath icy rain pelting down, wind blowing at increasing velocity. I told myself to be calm, though inwardly I was shaking. I knew the inflatable lifeboat was in the locker behind me. David was calm and spoke quietly throughout this ordeal. I never heard his voice change its timbre, and that was my comfort.

David was right; the Meltami didn't last long, maybe forty-five minutes, but it felt like twenty-four hours. For a few minutes after it passed David shook with cold. One friend put on the kettle for coffee, and we all warmed up and motored back to port. Forever after that fierce storm I've kept David's jacket close, on a hanger in my closet, a symbol of security, safe sailing, and maritime expertise.

In 1988, our third summer aboard *Bellatrix*, we headed for the islands of the Ionian Sea, where we would keep her for two years. A young couple, a son of a colleague of David's and his girlfriend, crewed for us from Reggio at the boot of Italy to Corfu. We arrived at night, having sailed past the coast of Albania, which was still under Communist rule. Fearing swimmers or small boats defecting to the freedom of the Greek shore, the Albanian government played search lights over the channel to pick up any brave defectors and sent out patrol boats to bring them back to jail.

Corfu City, the old harbor, was a small U-shaped harbor chock-a-block with sailing and motor craft and a smell to overwhelm even the most hardened nostrils. Arriving in darkness, we saw only the lights along the streets and harbor quays, but the overpowering odor of raw sewage and rotting food, stewed by the intense daily heat, bowled us over. Temperatures exceeded 100 degrees during the day, a fact not reported by the English newspaper as it would discourage British tourists.

But the city was beautiful. From the harbor we walked a winding street up the hill to the city center. Under Napoleon's rule the French had laid out Corfu City in a classical style around a large green Common. Restaurants, shops, some government buildings and the library overlooked the green. It reminded me of the Rue de Rivoli in Paris. The city combined the many customs and codes of its various rulers over several centuries: French, Italian, Ottoman, and British. Avoiding the odoriferous harbor, we ate many meals out of doors overlooking the Common, tasty combinations of antipasto, hummus, taramasalata, eggplant, and then fish and Greek salads, baklava, hot bitter chicory coffee.

At dusk we strolled around the Common, mingling with children at play and adults walking in a procession, a *passagiatta* down the street. On Sunday afternoons everyone watched the Corfiats play cricket, a sport harking back to the years of British control.

We sailed to some of the harbors to the north, St. Stephano, and to the southern outlying Islands, Paxos and Antipaxos. Lacca on Paxos was a charming village with a harbor for solid anchoring, diving off the bow, and rowing ashore in the dinghy.

And yet, always, homesickness plagued me; phoning once a week to my family from hotel lobbies and smoky bars frustrated me. Often during a conversation with one of my children or my mother, the line would cut off, and I could not reconnect. And the time differences disturbed me; in Italy we were nine and in Corfu ten hours from the West Coast of the U.S., almost a different day. In 1988 in Corfu City, I heard the news over a dirty black phone perched on top of a counter in a noisy smoky bar that Claire, my eldest granddaughter, aged five, had been diagnosed with Type 1 Diabetes. Chris did his best to reassure me that he and Lisa had found the best doctors in the San Francisco Bay area, and she was feeling better. No longer was she was dehydrated, she was eating well and ready for kindergarten in a few weeks.

Until I hung up I didn't cry, but then I fell into David's lap in inconsolable tears. The word diabetes carried lifetime concern, constant attention to sugar levels, insulin injections, and I could think of limits to Claire's expectations of an active life. I felt numb, desperately wishing I could hug her and Chris and Lisa. What would this mean to my darling granddaughter with the tumble of golden curls, and to her parents and baby brother, Sam. I tried to concentrate on the sailing activities, and our hosting friends on the boat, the daily sightseeing excursions around the island, the Roman ruins, and various other attractions. Time slowed down my anxiety and fears; they weren't as acute. Best yet, the following week I embraced Michael, my niece Jennifer and their friend Shelley at the Corfu airport. Michael consoled me and offered his healthy young perspective, hopeful, positive, that Chris and Lisa and Claire would deal with this, and indeed they have.

All summer we welcomed eager crews, who usually arrived on a Saturday and left on the next Friday, which gave us time to freshen the forward cabin and do the laundry before the next crew arrived. From Los Angeles came Michael and his team. From Singapore came David's niece Lucy and her husband, Colin. From Minneapolis came our friend, Lucia Morison, who had taken Greek lessons in order to converse with the Corfiats.

These visits were easy and joyful in spite of another Meltami during Michael and the girls' visit. It occurred right in the waters off Corfu City. Almost without a sign we were caught in a tempest. Michael, on deck with me and David, obeyed his command to pull out the inflatable lifeboat from the locker. Almost with one finger, flush with adrenalin, Michael executed the order. Soon it was over, but the girls never regained their enjoyment for boating in these waters.

Later David and I arranged to have lunch with a London friend, Mali de Robillant, at the villa she had taken on the cliff overlooking the San Stephano harbor. A young Italian woman was staying with her, a sort of Ophelia figure, fey, with long curling flaxen hair and dressed in layers of white gauze, her skirt brushing her bare feet. I thought she was on drugs since she spoke so peculiarly, vague and disconnected. She draped her long skinny arms over the table, extending herself towards David. His eyes lit up. But the conversation made no sense, and when I tried to enter, I discovered there was no entry point, just waves of words. At last I pushed back my chair and left the table, left the patio, searching for a bedroom to collect myself.

On my return as they were leaving the table, Mali told me that I shouldn't try to control David. Those were her precise words. I shrank. She was David's longtime friend, his interests were hers. But what could she mean? I hadn't uttered a word. At that moment I wished for nothing more than to be back in comfortable, understanding, familiar Minnesota.

Actually I had little time to sulk. Someone shouted that *Bellatrix* was moving from her anchor, drifting towards the harbor entrance. We quickly said goodbye and dashed for the shore, and David rowed our dinghy at high speed towards the boat. We climbed aboard to motor back to Corfu City. We never spoke about the lunch or about my abrupt departure from the table. David ignored these incidents. For him flirting was a game, an opportunity to resharpen his emotional arrows, a time to relish, and certainly not an occasion for spousal rehash and complaint. I learned to keep my feelings to myself, but I had never forgotten that evening so long ago when Eben and Sonia looked at each other with the gaze that had changed my life, and now understood I would be wary forever after.

In midsummer 1989 we delayed our departure for Corfu, as that was the year David suffered his first heart problem, atrial fibrillation. His health would slowly deteriorate. I knew things would never be the same. After that he began to tire more easily, and we needed friends about to assist us on windy seagoing passages. So that summer was quiet. David's other niece, Jane, and friend Ellie arrived for a few days followed by my brother and sister-in-law Ben and Joanie, who joined us for a week to cruise the islands south of Corfu. And in early September, David's daughter Virginia arrived with the Royal Yacht Squadron members for a week of club cruising around the islands. We had "done" the Ionian and looked forward to the next year's cruise to Dubrovnik and the Adriatic.

In May 1990 *Bellatrix* began her voyage northwards. Experienced crew, Ben and Rosalind Heywood, joined us for the leg from Corfu to Dubrovnik. We sailed all night to arrive in Dubrovnik at dawn. Without sleep we eagerly stepped ashore to investigate this old and revered city. The Saturday market was thriving. The sights and smells of the stalls; live animals, produce, exotic fruits and sweetmeats, and colorful woven goods aroused every sense and stayed with me as memories. But all too soon, the weekend was over, and we flew back to London.

Two months later, in early July, my father died quietly at home in his bedroom overlooking Lake Minnetonka. I flew to Minneapolis to join the rest of my family to attend his memorial service celebrating his active, vital years. We savored this time together. My sons and other male family members chose some of his tailored sport jackets and suits to take to their own closets, an ever-present memory of Dad's fine taste. On other occasions we would choose various books from his vast collection for our own libraries.

Within days I was back in London, and on August 1st, David and I rejoined *Bellatrix*. As in previous summers, family and friends met us in various ports to explore the tiny islands of the Dalmatian Coast. One night in Korcula, David and I were alone eating at an outdoor restaurant when he told me that the meat I was so enjoying was probably horse meat, considered a delicacy in this part of the world. David laughed at my distress, but from that moment on, I always ordered fish and my favorite calamari.

Sailing around the Ionian Islands; Polly with brother Ben and wife Joanie Case, 1989

In early September we secured *Bellatrix* in a new marina at Split in Croatia. The Croatians had developed and marketed a network of marinas all along the coast. They offered clean restrooms, grocery stores, marine shops, repairs and a good safe harbor. But as we prepared to leave Split we noticed increasing crowds of people entering the city, carrying banners, marching peacefully through the main streets, proclaiming statements over loud hailers. We thought this demonstration was a regional gathering, but we later learned we had witnessed the spark of the Croatian War, the first of the series of deadly Yugoslavian conflicts that would continue unabated over the ensuing years.

Tito surely would have turned over in his grave to behold his country erupting into sectarian strife. After World War II, he had kept all the disparate ethnic groups under tight control. After his death, the discipline and framework disintegrated as each group, Catholic, Protestant, and Muslim, exercised its will and independence. I never understood why anyone expected the nation to remain as an integral unit.

Along the Dalmation Coast, 1990

And during the winter of 1990-91 we watched, dismayed and horrified, as the Croatian War between Croatia and its German-leaning Catholic constituency and the central Protestant government in Zagreb erupted. Split was in the center of the bloody fighting. Although the navy yard behind the marina was bombed, fortunately for us, *Bellatrix* and her marina were left undamaged. Still that next summer the British government forbade travel to Yugoslavia, and we could not reach our boat. Occasionally the marina sent welcome news that *Bellatrix* was safe, but we spent our summer holidays in England sailing on the Solent, and I began my search in Cheshire for my Quaker ancestors.

In the spring of 1992, war still raging, David arranged for a Dutchman and a Croatian to sail *Bellatrix* across the Adriatic to a small port of San Giorgio. When she arrived she was in good order but filthy, and David's brand-new sailing jacket had disappeared, a small price to pay for a boat completely intact.

We didn't know it then, but this was to be our final year on *Bellatrix*. We both agreed that we were not as physically able as we had been six years earlier, and we had exceeded our five-year plan. Now we needed crew even for routine passages. The time had come to sell her. And so it was a summer of celebration as friends arrived to cruise up the east coast of Italy. From across the Adriatic we frequently heard sounds of artillery fire punching the air, though the Italian Coast was remarkably peaceful as we made our way to Rimini, Pessaro, finally Chiaggio and the Grand Canal and Venice.

Thanks to David's British yacht club membership, we moored at a tiny harbor across from San Marco, marveling in every direction at the splendid sights of Venice. We spent two weeks enjoying Venice, never leaving the harbor as we feared losing our berth. We took the *vaporetti* throughout the city. I slung laundry bags over my shoulders for the ride to a laundry in a commercial section, and both of us explored churches and markets. One weekend the Canal teemed with gondolas gathered for an annual race, but once again, too soon, our summer was over, and we motored our boat towards

Trieste and a Westerly company secondhand boat sale. We scrubbed and polished *Bellatrix*, said farewell, and flew back to London. Within days *Bellatrix* was sold, and though we felt sad, we were proud to learn that someone valued her as we did.

David kept a log of all those *Bellatrix* years, and I refer to various places and incidents he noted, relishing especially the memories of the years before David developed his heart trouble, the years when he was so vital he could handle the boat single-handedly—although I was mighty quick with mooring lines and anchor. But he could have done it all. After 1989 he gradually slowed. When we had moored in a small harbor with guests aboard, we often talked during lunch in the cockpit about exploring the nearby town. David would tell us to go ahead, that he was happy aboard the boat, which I translated to mean "I really want to take a nap." So the guests and I jumped onto the quay to wend our way through cobbled streets, markets, and dark, dank churches with their ever-present images of the Virgin Mary and the tiny candles parishioners lit to remember loved ones. Back on board we'd find David restored and ready for tea or a drink in the cockpit and the evening ahead.

Photographs of each of those sailing summers fill David's scrapbooks. He loved to capture the harbor scenes, the boats and their rigs, the some eccentrically-dressed skippers, the bollards and distinctive features of a harbor village, a market, and a tiny church. He photographed our various crew members at the helm or a group enjoying a meal in the cockpit. The books tell the real stories of those years and the joy we enjoyed together on *Bellatrix*.

# To Cranmer Court

We were beginning to feel cramped in David's bachelor flat. We didn't acknowledge that we were, but our friends kept asking why we weren't moving to a larger flat. We replied that we felt no urgency, we relished our intimacy. We had easily adjusted our spaces, enjoyed securing our possessions in small spaces, carefully discarding and giving to charity those items unlikely to be used again. In many ways, David said, it was like living on a boat, which inspired us with thoughts of adventure and pleasure.

But after I left my Bryanston Square office and brought my files home, we were crowded. I hadn't realized how much space I would need for my personal material. I needed more room for scrapbooking and for research and writing my Quaker book. I bought the essential laptop computer, attached an extension cord and plugged it into a socket next to our square table where I worked, but compromising space and moving for meals began to pall.

Finding another flat that suited us aesthetically, physically, and financially was difficult. David and I agreed that we wouldn't move far from the Chelsea Green. With little enthusiasm we looked over the weekend papers' listings and set off to view available flats in nearby neighborhoods. No flat seemed right; windows were too high or too few, or street parking spaces were inadequate, or the surroundings were indifferent. In truth we didn't want to move.

David suggested we should consider a flat in Cranmer Court, where he had been living when we met, should one become available. So, he spread the word around the Green and among the residents of Cranmer Court that we were interested. Almost immediately the owner of David's former flat contacted us to say he wished to sell. His children who were living there needed a larger family house in the country.

The flat was about half again as large as ours, spacious rooms with thirteen windows facing south lighting even the dimmest gray day, a small additional bathroom, and more closets. The second bedroom would be my office. The living room windows were large and looked out over the Tudor dwellings on Whiteheads' Grove. The kitchen could accommodate several people. Our flat was on the fourth floor, five floors above street level. Although there was a lift, David said that we must adhere to his former practice of walking up the stairs to keep in shape. So we made a pact that we would not use the lift unless we were carrying heavy sacks of groceries or suitcases.

We were thrilled to remain in the neighborhood and return to David's former residence where there was excellent porterage and a long-standing association to manage our property.

So we began negotiations and arrived at a price that suited both parties. David put me in charge of the process. I was to sell our present flat and organize the move to Cranmer Court. Selling our flat required inspectors to confirm the building's integrity, scrutinizing the quality of the brickwork, heating, and roofing. We found a buyer and agreed on a price. Unfortunately when the inspectors reported that the exterior brick work needed repointing, we had to lower the price. Then the sale was solid. I arranged for us to remain an extra month in our old flat to allow time for painters to apply a fine coat of lustrous white to most of the walls, soon to be covered with David's paintings.

And so on May 1st, 1992, we moved from Elystan Place around the block to Cranmer Court to place our furniture and paintings and personal possessions in their new locations. In my

View of Chelsea Green from
our kitchen window,
Cranmer Court, 1992

office room, now painted a brilliant marigold, I arranged a fine old
desk of David's mother's, a built-in counter and shelf and a pull-
out couch to accommodate guests and seating for prospective
Smith College students I would interview. Many of these young
women were studying at the American school in St. John's Wood
near Regent's Park or at international schools in the London area.
I first visited the schools to promote my college and then con-
ducted the interviews in my "Room of One's Own."

As we gained more space, I expanded my volunteer projects,
I could write and organize my book and remain in my little room
while David occupied the sitting room, at his desk in the south-
west corner surrounded by his scrapbooks and CDs and files. It

Formally attired for a summer wedding, London, 1990

seemed ideal, but in this larger space, we were losing our closeness. We didn't collide, we didn't bump, we didn't have to negotiate personal space. We could operate along parallel lines without announcing our plans, we could go through our daily routines along our separate highways. I could close the door of my room and talk on the phone without being overheard and use my new internet and e-mail capability to plan tennis games and other activities with my girlfriends, or investigate travel costs for a quick trip to the U.S. without previously discussing these ideas with David, and he could arrange his own daily life on the phone at his desk.

Instead of David's voice a few feet from me, I shouted down the hall from our bedroom to the kitchen, "What did you say?" We laughed together but we were apart. And other chores changed also. Now that we had a washer and dryer unit in the kitchen we no longer combined efforts to sort and fill our laundry bags to take to Rose. Use of the bathroom was unimpeded, convenient but reducing the communication about rightful occupancy. I rose before David, put on a bathrobe and ate my breakfast in the kitchen listening to Radio 3 morning news while he was at the other end of the flat enjoying a few more moments in bed. Our large Pullman-car flat, compared to our square box, with each quarter a tiny room, was pulling us apart. As we had no dishwasher, we continued our practice of washing the dishes and glasses in the morning. I washed the plates and David the glasses. Now with the kitchen at the end of the flat, I could get away with washing the glasses before I washed the plates, and inadvertently denied David his task. He complained but I laughed it off, and it wasn't until he was ill and confronted me that I realized I had taken away kitchen routines he enjoyed.

The large square table surrounded by three sofas dominated the center of the living/ sitting room. David often spread out his current scrapbook on the table and worked at it throughout the day. During our evenings at home, I brought my current book from a shelf in my "Room of One's Own" to sit and cut and paste across from him. These cozy evenings reminded me of our evenings at Elystan Place.

Although we relished our spacious quarters, I felt that in many ways, we had established independent patterns to our lives. We had relinquished an intimacy that we would not recover.

# Closing Down

David retired in his sixty-fifth year, a few months after we married. He said firmly that he was through working, through "doing things at someone else's behest." He would not accept any consulting work. The insurance industry was changing, the familiar "old boy" networks were disappearing, and he felt soon his expertise would be obsolete. I did not agree. I thought that he would be stimulated and rise to a new challenge, and conversely that he would languish physically and mentally without some professional responsibility. I didn't think retirement was healthy for him, he needed more regular activity than sailing and walking.

I was right, as it happened. His health began to fail, or as he described it, "the edifice is crumbling." His doctor had told him to watch his weight, but since he had no idea of the basic food groups and no interest in learning, he didn't know what foods to eat or avoid. But recently he had asked me to monitor his craving for chocolate; ice cream, cake, and, in fact, all sweets. His idea of a perfect menu was a meal starting with dessert, or pudding as it's known in the U.K.

After Dr. Pigott diagnosed atrial fibrillation and tried an unsuccessful electric shock to the heart, he prescribed pills and again cautioned about weight gain. In 1997, eight years after the original diagnosis, David suffered two rigid fainting spells, at the Fourth of

July parade in Edgartown, Martha's Vineyard, and several weeks later at a concert at Royal Albert Hall in London.

The Fourth of July incident is burned into my memory. We were visiting American friends from business days. On a sweltering hot afternoon we stood at a neighbor friend's fence in the heart of Edgartown. I had chosen to drink water instead of wine or a gin and tonic, but David could not resist his favorites. The traditional holiday parade began with town dignitaries, Boy and Girl Scout troops, veterans of foreign wars, members of the D.A.R., all marching to the trumpets and clarinets of the local brass band.

All of a sudden I looked at David standing by my side, and I saw he was absolutely rigid, speechless, stiff, clinging to the fence. I thought immediately that he'd had a stroke, and I called to Peter Guernsey, our host. We loosened his grip on the fence and slowly lowered his unconscious body to the ground. How many minutes was he out? Who knows, but it seemed a very long time. He slowly came around, blinking and unsure of where he was. Within minutes, fortunately, the Edgartown firemen, waving from their open fire truck, appeared in the parade, and I ran out on the street to signal them to come to David's aid. Several fireman quickly attended him and called an ambulance.

The parade stopped, people politely kept their distance, and I mopped his face with a damp cloth and spoke reassuringly to him as he became more aware of his plight. The ambulance arrived to take us to the hospital, about a five-minute ride.

The Emergency Room team gave him several tests and pronounced him well enough to be released. But the doctor advised us to return to London as soon as possible for further tests for his heart problem. That suddenly, illness had struck. I had planned to visit family on the West Coast and David was to sail with friends to Nova Scotia. With this change of course, I was struck by a wave of selfish homesickness. My grandchildren were growing up, and though here and there I managed a weekend trip from London to watch them running for touchdowns, dribbling soccer balls, racing down slalom ski hills, gracefully taking a horse over a jump, or hitting a home run, I was sad that this visit to watch a summer slalom race had to be canceled.

I had no way of knowing then, of course, that this was to be the first of many emergency trips to the hospital by ambulance. On July 6th we returned to the U.K. and David began undergoing a battery of tests. The doctor concluded this rigid faint was a heart phenomenon exacerbated by alcohol. He advised new medicines and no further drinking, and David did try to abide by the doctor's instructions. Unfortunately when he ignored the warnings, the results were dramatic.

Five weeks after the Fourth of July incident, we accepted an invitation to a Proms Concert and seats in one of the Royal boxes at Royal Albert Hall. Our hosts served wine, Perrier water and sandwiches before the concert. David drank the wine but ignored the food. The concert began. There we were, front and center; I was sitting behind him and saw his shoulders stiffen. I jumped over the person in the seat in front of me, grasped David, pushed him to the ground just as the doctor had instructed this to permit blood to flow to his head. Soon he came around, but we had already alerted the emergency team in the concert hall, and the ambulance was on its way. During the interval, under the watchful gaze of audience members in the main hallway, we exited. After this evening, David began to pay attention to the warnings.

No doubt he was more tired, a bit scared. I could tell this because from time to time, he became anxious and abrupt with me. He did not understand or care about the details of his illness, and so he depended on my understanding his predicament, and yet he resented my showing too much knowledge. He didn't want me to boss him around, so I trod cautiously, trying to encourage him to eat and drink properly.

During these years my mother's health deteriorated. She had suffered a major stroke in 1991, a year after my father's death, and, although cheerful and alert, she was wheelchair-bound for the rest of her life. I tried to visit her several times a year, usually after a visit to the children on the West Coast. With 'round-the-clock care Mother lived in the family home until the fall of 1998, when she transferred to a local nursing home.

At the same time my sister contracted ovarian cancer. Rounds of chemotherapy brought remission for several months but the cancer returned in September 1999. CC bravely tended to her family and supervised Mother's care at the nursing home. Surrounded by Ben, CC, and me, Mother died peacefully a few days before Christmas that year. And then, the following June, CC died. Within months of each other, I lost my mother and my sister.

I could only put one foot in front of the other, pressing my grief deep down inside me as I now had to focus on David's bladder cancer. On the last Friday in May in London when David was undergoing biopsies to confirm his cancer, CC had phoned to inform me her doctor told her she had less than a month to live. Several days later after I settled David at home in our flat, I flew to Minneapolis to stay in a small condominium we had purchased to be close to CC until her death. After her funeral, I flew back to London to care for David. I write these sentences matter-of-factly. Even now, if I dwell on the pressures and the stress and the emotions of that summer and subsequent months, I am profoundly sad.

David began chemotherapy, which was ineffective, but radiation treatments gave him a remission for more than a year. Then, on a Sunday evening in mid-January 2002, he contracted a bladder infection. I called 999 for an ambulance to transport us to the Chelsea and Westminster hospital. That infection led to problems with other organs which hospitalized him for the winter months, and then a CAT scan revealed the final story. Bone cancer had spread throughout his body. His doctor gave him a few days to live; he lived for six, peacefully medicated on morphine.

During those days as David slipped slowly into a coma, I rarely left his bedside. He talked softly, remembering the parts of our life together that he had especially enjoyed, our sailing trips, the concerts we attended, and the times with both our families. As he wandered in and out of his comas, I sat beside him reliving our most intimate years in his Elystan Place flat. It was during these days that, I told him, I could never forget:

Your face as it always was to me at Elystan Place, your laughing eyes and mouth greeting me each evening as I returned from work, opening the door to the postage-stamp-sized hallway. Your face as it was in each doorway opening into the hallway with a long mirror to catch an image, at any time of the day.

Your face from the kitchen, preparing a dish for a dinner party, eager, full of creative joy as you smashed the juniper berries to coat the chicken in the clay brick, giving it that special flavor. You loved all that cooking, sipping a vodka as you went along. You hated to give it all up when you got sick.

Your face from the sitting room as you got up from the square center table or your desk doing the scrapbooks or placing a tape on the machine. Your face in triumph as you located with a flashlight your favorite blue suit among all the other blues in the small dark closet behind a sofa.

Your face from the bedroom, the morning light behind you as you always gleefully began each day, the television blaring with the morning news or you selecting a bright tie from the desk drawer. Your face in the evening, eager and loving, as you drew me onto our bed.

Your face from the loo, the bathroom, covered with shaving soap, calling out some hilarious word, some suggestions for the day or for the upcoming evening. Your face with hair neatly combed or tilting your head, parting your hair and smoothing it down. You were vain—combs everywhere, below the car's dashboard, jackets, desk drawer, at the back of the chart table on *Bellatrix*. You always wore a coat and tie in London and said each time we went out in the evening, "How do I look?" You might notice my dress, or maybe not.

Elystan Place was it. There then was no separation between us, no room for differing agendas. Elystan Place was whole, it was us. The center of our lives around the square table, the sofas, the lamps, the paintings on every wall space, the books surrounding us in neat piles or in bookcases, but not crowding us, rather illuminating, enriching, providing but not curtailing or suffocating. This was our happiest, most entwined, reciprocal, most linked life. It was the core of our closeness.

My reveries slipped away as he opened his eyes and looked at me, lifting his arms. "Come into my arms," he said as he tried to muster strength to give me a hug. I snuggled close and opened his hospital gown to rest my head on his bare chest. There it was, the scent of crushed basil leaves, and again I remember discovering this unique smell during our early nights together. And then it became even more pungent during our summer sailing. From morning to evening, the hot sun bathed us in steaming rays. Standing beside him in the boat's cockpit I could feel the temperature rising as the scent rose from his body. That smell was a seductive sensuous smell, not an acrid sweaty odor but warm and compelling as if his body were infused with the herbs and breezes of the Mediterranean and the pine trees ashore.

In London, too, during the shortening dark days of autumn, the damp cold days of winter, and the fresh days of spring, I inhaled this scent. So I discovered it was an inner body warmth that manufactured this peculiar odor, a combination of ingredients that burst forth in a compelling invitation to come closer, to burrow into his chest, inhale, receive a message of intoxication, understand the beauty of soul. As he lay dying, I murmured, "You always smell so good."

David died on March 13 that year.  2002

And after his children and I had said farewell and talked about the funeral arrangements, I returned to our flat filled with David's treasures. I walked the rooms, gazing at the memorabilia and paintings, prints and his Victorian scrapbooks, for which he had won a prize years before for the brilliant and witty collection and mounting of the social and political clippings of the day and his own skillfully composed photographs. I looked at his wooden boat models, remembering he had designated one for a grandson. And there was his collection of CDs, a mélange of classical music,

David on Caribbean holiday, 1998

and jazz, mostly Baroque compositions—Bach, Mozart, Handel—
and his beloved Fats Waller and Duke Ellington. Soon bouquets
of flowers arrived, filling tables and desktops in the sitting room
and bedroom, and the fragrance of stargazer lilies permeated every room. Best of all, my son Charlie arrived to provide support
from my family, and we joined David's family to celebrate his life
at a service at St. Luke's Church just off the Chelsea Green. We
sang loudly and clearly familiar hymns, "~~From~~ For All the Saints,"
"Eternal Father Strong to Save," "I Danced in the Morning," and
we marched resolutely from the sanctuary to a rousing organ rendition of "When the Saints Go Marching In."

At the reception in the church vestry, the questions came.

"Are you going back to the States?" "Will you be leaving?" "Is England home now?"

"No, no," I said firmly. "I'm not leaving. How could I leave you all?"

"Yes, this is home."

During the months of David's deteriorating health and hospitalizations I felt tied to London, and to my life with David. I couldn't concentrate on anything but that life; every day I focused on his well-being, at home, and in the ambulance, in the Emergency Room, the wards, and finally in a private hospital room. Buoyed by his spirit and the daily calls from friends and family, I felt firmly embedded in London; that city was my cocoon, the place I felt at peace and comforted. I sincerely believed that I would remain at Cranmer Court after David's death, and that I would only travel back and forth to the States.

After David's funeral, back at our flat, Charlie asked me if I would stay on, and I gave him the same answer I'd given everyone. I simply had not for a moment thought of packing up and returning to my roots.

For the first weeks after his funeral, I was busy making arrangements for scattering his ashes, and the weekdays were as always busy. But my weekends felt long and shapeless. Friends and family had other plans. I was a widow, alone and on my own, and it was up to me to make the best of a London weekend.

I realized I didn't know how to do that, and time weighed heavily. I carefully planned daytime excursions and Saturday evening theater performances in the West End. I combed the newspapers searching for the interesting exhibitions at the London galleries and museums, and I set off on foot and via underground, working to keep busy. I forced myself to attend to the paintings and sculpture I saw, to be alert to new artists coming on the scene and to revisit some of my old favorites at the National Gallery. On Sundays, after church, I read the papers and waited impatiently for my family in California and Oregon to wake for my phone call to them.

For London residents Sundays are family days, days to visit the country together or to enjoy a lingering lunch, and so after I placed my calls, I would wander outside and take long walks through our neighborhood, usually winding up at friends' houses where I would join them for an evening drink.

But then I had to return home, and each time I entered our flat I felt David's presence. It overwhelmed me. All those paintings he had bought so carefully over the years, his scrapbooks by his desk, his desk just as it was when he left that last time for the hospital—the leather box for letters, matching blotter and polished steel winch from a favorite sailboat. Everywhere I turned I saw and felt and smelled and heard David. His clothes and "objets" were everywhere—in closets, bureau drawers, displayed on shelves and on the mantel. I was not yet ready to sort out his things, far from ready to give them away. And so they remained, a reminder of the man who was no longer there.

Even stepping outside wasn't much easier. Our neighborhood carried his memories. I looked about me and remembered why I was there, this woman from middle America living in this building just off the Chelsea Green. I couldn't enter a shop without thinking of him; there was the picture framer who was repairing one of David's oil paintings, the chemist who had so promptly and sympathetically filled every prescription, Rose, the laundress, who shook her head each time I passed her window, the greengrocer who had brought a basket of fruit to the hospital, and the delicatessen where David bought his sausage or smoked salmon for lunch.

Watching the buses trundling down the Kings Road, I couldn't stop thinking of riding with David, of the two of us sitting on the top deck so we could see the carved stone pediments set in the tops of the buildings. And after he became frail and couldn't climb the bus stairs, sitting up front on the lower deck. Now I simply felt better on the underground.

# A Sailor's Ashes

Looking at my 2002 diary to those weeks after David's death, I see almost every night filled with dinner or theater and opera engagements. Everyone of our friends or family took great pains to keep me busy. I don't remember regretting an invitation. I played tennis at least twice a week at the Queen's or Vanderbilt Tennis clubs with my long-standing tennis group. After the game, we often played a few hands of bridge. I woke each morning with a schedule of activity, but I knew that when I returned to our flat I would know that I was alone. No cheery voice called out, "Hello, Darling."

On a blustery early May morning I walked towards the mortuary, holding the leather handle of David's small navy blue canvas bag. Along the Fulham Road, opposite the Chelsea and Westminster Hospital where David had died, stood the Chelsea Funeral home, a white stucco building marked by two white pillars at the doorway. As I walked into the front office, one of the black-suited directors came forward to help me.

"Have you taken good care of him?" I asked. The director said nothing.

"I'm talking about my husband, David Grose," I said.

"Yes, Madam," he said. "Are you here to collect the ashes?"

"Yes," I said. "I'm here to collect my husband."

"Very well." He turned and pushed aside a purple curtain to

enter another room, then quickly returned holding a large maroon-colored plastic urn. As he placed it on the counter, he asked coolly, "Where will Mr. Grose be interred?"

"I'll scatter his ashes on the Beaulieu River near Southampton."

"Very well, Madam," he said, his face a mask of indifference. "To open the urn, you will need to cut the tape around the rim, and then inside you will remove an inner cap protecting the ashes."

"What if the wind is blowing?" I asked him. I had never questioned David's desire to have his ashes scattered at sea, but now I was feeling anxiety about unforeseen problems.

"You will need to be careful to scatter downwind," he spoke through a row of very fine teeth. "Now, Madam, everything's in order," he said, and he offered me the urn.

"It's so heavy," I said, pulling it to my chest, startled by the weight of this plastic container.

"Yes, Madam."

I thanked him and placed the urn in the small bag, turned and opened the door to the street. I was grateful for the sun's warmth as the east wind swirled around me. I walked home along the streets so familiar from my daily trips to the hospital. On the corner of Old Church Street I passed the flower stall, flush with spring tulips, daffodils, and iris. I had often bought bouquets of these flowers to bring color and fragrance to David's hospital room. This day, I had the urn to carry home. Perhaps I'd buy myself some flowers later at the Chelsea Green. I crossed the street to South Parade, past the cheerful Colombier Restaurant where the two of us had so often enjoyed delicious Beef Bourguignon and crême brulée. I quickly stepped past the Royal Marsden Cancer Hospital, home of David's many chemotherapy and radiation treatments, and around the corner to cross Sidney Street and straight ahead along Cale street to the Chelsea Green that bustled with the activity of a midweek spring morning. The ironmonger had arranged some tools and pots outside his doorway, and the greengrocer had placed pails of fresh flowers at the entrance to his shop. I called out to the proprietor that I would be back later for some tulips.

I shifted the bag from one hand to the other. I was almost home. I longed to put the urn down and prepare myself for tomorrow. I had to shake off the anxiety I was feeling. Probably sadness as this moment approached. I entered our building and took the lift to our floor.

Someone had warned me the urn would be heavy—yes, I remembered, but I couldn't remember who that someone was. Whoever said it had told me I would have to concentrate, work to hold it firmly when I tipped it to scatter David's ashes.

I sat down on the living room sofa. Ah, yes, I remembered then. It was Judy; several years earlier she had scattered her Philip's ashes. Judy was a sturdy woman, larger, far stronger than I, an experienced sailor who could cast an anchor off the bow as if it were a pillow. If Judy thought the urn was heavy, how would I do? How awful to drop it, let it slip from my hands over the side into the foaming wake as the boat circled the river water. All of David's ashes tumbling into the churning water, all at once, without even a prayer or a song. Yes, Judy had told me what I must do. I flexed my hands. I would hold the urn fast and safely. I would.

It was lunchtime. I fixed a small salad and a few pieces of rye krisp, and I knew I had to think about other things this afternoon. I bought the tulips and walked to the Library, and to Peter Jones, the department store in Sloane Square, to buy some sheer tights to wear that evening to David's son-in-law Johnny Polk's sixtieth birthday party. Thank goodness for that diversion.

But before I could dress for the party, I had an important task to perform. I carried the urn into my small study. There I placed a square white table cloth on the floor and arranged kitchen scissors, a large silver dessert spoon, and David's favorite olive-wood box around the urn in the center of the cloth. I knelt on the floor to cut the tape, pulled off the lid, and gently removed the inner cap. There they were, David's ashes, mingled with bits of bone and gristle, parts of my husband's body that had failed to disintegrate in the flame, David's oatmeal-colored, textured remains.

I leaned over and studied them. David's ashes.

What bits of bone were these? I gently reached in—were these bits of his elbow? Those elbows that had bent to the rhythm of the oars as he expertly rowed our dinghy from the mooring to the Southampton Yacht Club dock. Were these his fingers, the bones of his hands that had held me, that had reached for me during the night, had touched my fingers, moving softly, rubbing up and down my wrist as he lay in his London hospital bed, days from death? Alive, my husband's hands were warm, his clasp firm, at least until that final morphine-induced coma. I could feel his touch.

And here? Perhaps these were the bits of his arms, the muscular arms that hoisted the mainsail without straining, without a pause, hoisted while his eyes watched to make sure the sail traveled properly up the mast.

David had had good solid Cornish bones, and here they were, mostly ash and bones I carefully measured out with a dessert spoon, filling the box. When I had moved remnants of my husband into this box that I would take with me to the States, I fastened the lid and secured it with tape. I would pour these ashes into Lake Minnetonka just off the marina dock where David so often had watched the remodeled streetcar boat dropping off its passengers. There, several blocks from our small condominium on the main street of Wayzata, some part of David would rest, close to me in the place I called my homeland.

I placed the olive-wood box in my top bureau drawer and returned the urn to the hall table.

It was time to dress for Johnny's party. I chose a bright red silk dress and clasped my grandmother's strand of luminous pearls around my neck. I felt I looked a bit too dressy for the underground, so I splurged on a taxi cab for the short ride to Christie's, one of London's leading art auction houses, located off St. James's Square. Many of Bino and Johnny's friends and our family were gathered in the large first-floor galleries for the cocktail party. I moved from group to group chatting and sipping several classes of Veuve Clicquot. People hugged and kissed and told me how pretty I looked. I smiled, knowing the dress fit perfectly. Several months before he became ill, David had asked our local dressmaker to design a couture cocktail dress. I felt exhilarated and warmed by friendship, and when I returned home and turned on all the lights, I felt less lonely, comforted by the evening's pleasure.

Early the next morning David's family and I drove in several cars to the Beaulieu River. The sun was sharp, not a cloud in the sky, the river rippling in an easterly breeze, not brisk, but consistent, a breeze David would have enjoyed. As the tide turned and began its sweep out the river to the Solent and on to the English Channel, I climbed aboard the yacht club dinghy and took a seat in the stern. Linden, the boatman, sat next to me and soon he was moving the tiller, pointing us from the mooring dock to the main stream.

I looked at David's three daughters and his sister, Molly, and Richard Ford, our longtime sailing mate, beside me in the stern. They were making light conversation about the luck of a sunny day and the pleasant breeze. Robert, the club manager and a boat man himself, was also aboard, but he seemed subdued. Robert and Lin loved David, had for so long enjoyed exchanging playful barbs each weekend as we prepared to set sail. I knew they would miss their friend.

Our destination was the mouth of the river. I clasped the urn in both hands. At my feet lay the handbag where I had stashed wads of Kleenex and a prayer of Commitment at Sea scrawled by our minister on a piece of paper. He had told me this was the prayer to use, the prayer that would make this act official, solemn, and bring permanent rest to the departed and comfort to the bereaved.

I faced straight ahead, vaguely listening to the others' chatter, aware that David's family was making the best of this ritual, that they were sad but comfortable. It had been almost two months since his death; it was time to rest his ashes. How lucky to have a bright, sunlit day and warm temperatures. I felt grateful for that at least, and grateful to have his loving family and friends along.

And then within ten minutes, we reached the mouth of the river, and Linden said, "This is it."

Everyone grew quiet as Lin began to turn the boat in a slow circle. This was the moment, I knew. I stood to kneel over the side of the dinghy, and as I adjusted myself, I felt the urn begin to slip. My skin prickled, I felt a strain in my neck. Oh no, hang on, girl, I thought. Keep going. You'll be okay. I thought of David and his frequent praise for my poise and strength. I wouldn't let him down.

I lifted the urn as best I could, and I began to pour. I tried to spill the ashes evenly as Lin continued to circle. David's daughters, Virginia and Talia, stood to toss bouquets of violets and daffodils into the water's circle, and as they did I glimpsed their straight backs and their hair, one blonde, one dark, blowing in the wind.

I poured and poured. How many ashes and gristle made up this body? He had not been a large man, my husband, but there seemed to be so much of him here, so much more than I'd imagined there would be.

I held fast, pouring a steady stream. I knew this could not be easy for the others, though I couldn't look away from that flowing stream. Tears ran down my face, and I sniffled loudly, but I continued to pour, and as the urn became lighter, I tipped it up on end to complete the stream.

And it was over.

All of David, except for the spoonfuls in the olive-wood box, had entered the mouth of the Beaulieu River, the mouth that had been the site of our adventures, of our home away from home, the site where David had for so many years traveled in and out, in and out, and now forever he would rest on the seabed among seaweed, grasses, rocks, and silt, that rich carpet supporting his happiest days.

My job was over.

I stood and pulled the prayer from my bag, wiped my face of tears and began to read. I had to read slowly to keep from crying, but then I couldn't help myself, and I read through tears, the words as thick and muddy as the river bottom. But I knew they were clear to the others, and I didn't stop reading until I reached the end of the prayer.

"Receive him into this cool water and into the arms
of your mercy, into the blessed company of everlasting
peace, and into the glorious company of the saints
in light."

When I finished, hands reached out to hold mine, and a hug came from somewhere. I felt unburdened. I had followed David's instructions, had done him proud—one of his expressions. I had met the challenge, and although I could not stop crying, I let the sun and the warmth of those hands comfort me.

As Linden turned the dinghy upstream towards the yacht club, I clutched the empty urn.

David was gone, and all I had left was this horrible plastic urn. Let it go! I thought. And I remembered then that I wasn't holding it but I've no idea where that monstrous thing went. Did I give it to Richard or to Robert to toss into the dumpster? I don't remember, but suddenly it was gone.

Back at the yacht club we thanked Robert and Linden and I hugged them both, and as I did I knew deep down that I was un-likely to see them again. I would have no reason to visit the club, no reason to relive our sailing life on the Beaulieu. I couldn't. If the tears didn't flow down my cheeks, they would still slosh in my wind-pipe. I must move on, come to grips with a life without David.

Over the side I had sent him, just like that, a steady stream of him. "Over the side," he had so often chanted as he tossed a rusty tool, a bottle or a tin, into the water. He never gave a thought to polluting. The tide would take care of that, he said. Of course, it didn't. The rusty spanner was sitting atop fathoms-deep seabed alongside broken wooden chests spilling jewels from a wrecked Spanish cargo ship, or the Titanic's state-of-the-art navigational instruments. These remnants of a sailing life shifting, crumbling, with the sands and the rocks of the seabed tumbling with David's remains.

After we had left the club our little band drove to a nearby restaurant for a glass of champagne and lunch. My invitation, my lunch, David's lunch, my need to close the circle, to let him know that we would remember him always, reassure him that we had followed his wishes. "Over the side."

As the waiter cleared our first dishes, prawns on toast, I looked out the window. Cumulus clouds sifting through the bright blue sky, and memories washed over me. I thought of our cruises on the glorious Mediterranean, Ionian, and Adriatic, our days spent here on the Solent, misty, drizzly mornings when we swallowed cups of instant coffee, pulled on our jeans, jerseys, and oilskins, and set off.

At first light, that's when we always set off, leaving the mooring just as the dawn was about to break, heading to Yarmouth or Cowes, to St. Tropez, Bandol, Cogolin, along the coast of Tuscany, Porto Ercole, or the Ionian Sea, to Corfu, St. Stephano, or Trogir, Kortula, to the east coast of Italy, Rimini, Pesaro, and Venice.

Richard broke my reverie.

"You know I have one regret," he said.

I looked at him. His eyes were dry, but I could hear the emotion in his voice. "What's that?" I asked.

"I never sailed with you in the Med. You asked me every year and I never got there."

I nodded. "I know. Those were such wonderful years."

Suddenly I was looking out the window not at the Beaulieu River, but at the warm seas of the south of France, Italy, Corfu and the Dalmatian Coast.

# Return to My Roots

I had planned to spend two months of the summer at our condominium on the shores of Lake Minnetonka, just west of Minneapolis and within striking range of my children on the West Coast. I would return to London for Clarissa Post's wedding in mid-July. Peggy and Herschel Post, Clarissa's parents, were some of my closest friends.

But in mid-May, just before my departure, I began to imagine London in August, with most of my friends and David's family on holiday out of the country or staying at their country houses. London would be virtually empty then, and if time had felt empty in the spring, what would I feel like during those dog days of August? No, I wouldn't stay in London after the wedding. With bonus "air miles" I would fly back for another month in Minnesota.

On a bright May 18th, Patrick, our Irish porter, carried my bags from the flat to the front door of our building and hailed a taxi to take me to Victoria Station, where I would catch the express train to Gatwick Airport. My mind swirled with confusing emotions. Over the years our Cranmer Court porters had given us unstinting service, and especially in the last months of David's life during those frightening episodes when he fell to the floor, or couldn't move, or his fever soared. Always one of the porters responded immediately, helping me lift and comfort him as we waited for the ambulance and the all-too-frequent ride to the Emergency Room at the Chelsea and Westminster hospital.

My throat tightened as I said goodbye, and I didn't understand why I was fighting back tears. I would see Patrick in two months. He waved to me, and waved again. Did we both sense that I was beginning my permanent journey back to America? I think perhaps we did. My spirits lifted when the plane landed in Minneapolis, and before I even knew what was happening my calendar was filled with tennis and bridge dates, a writing course, and cocktail and supper parties on patios decorated with pots of geraniums, lobelia, and begonias. The Guthrie's summer season had begun. Arthur Miller was in residence writing *Resurrection Blues*, which was to premiere in early August. I slipped easily into a lively pattern of activity. Everyone seemed happy to see me, supportive and affectionate. I gave several small parties on my deck. I felt comfortable entertaining. I understood my roots in this world were deep and robust.

Too soon it was mid-July and time to return to London and Clarissa's wedding in Switzerland. Except for the wedding dance, I enjoyed the two-day celebration. But when the dancing commenced I slipped away, and walked up a short street to the hotel. Widows, and as I remembered divorced women, are extra baggage on a dance floor. Not a threat, just redundant. I entered the hotel and was surprised to see my friend Angela Fenhalls sitting at a table in the lounge ordering a glass of wine. Her husband was back in London; we could share our feelings about the predicaments of single women at a dance.

But there was more to that discussion. Widows were more respectable than divorcées; of course, widows endured a real loss, a husband was dead. Whatever loss one felt leaving a divorced partner, it wasn't the same as a deceased husband. But the loss to divorce of someone one loved was lingeringly painful, perhaps a loss one would never forget. Death was closure. There was a sense of failure and apologies about divorce while widowhood brought forth sympathy and understanding, and an outpouring of invitations to take up any lonely moments.

A day later I flew back to Minnesota, and as the summer came to its end, I talked with a friend about the future, about my homesickness, about the strength of my roots, about my growing feelings of separation from London. She told me firmly that I must listen to myself, that we have one life and need to take care of ourselves. Her words were comforting, insightful, and welcome.

As I boarded the airplane back to London, I felt a sense of peace wash over me; I was ready to make a decision. A steady flow of events, moments, and memories had slowly pushed me towards that decision, and then came the final push.

I could no longer avoid sorting through David's clothes. Fatima, our dear Portuguese cleaning lady, helped me, and I gingerly opened his closet to the tier of shelves filled with laundered shirts in their plastic wraps and cardboard collar holders. Above these were the sweaters, the wool jerseys, for London and sailing wear, and to the right of these the hanging section, navy blue jackets and trousers, one or two gray flannel trousers, and his brown tweed sport jacket, for Sunday lunch in the country. All those blue suits. David had used a flashlight to distinguish one jacket or pair of trousers from the other—the serge, the silk, the striped, the light wool, his wedding suit with the patched elbows. As soon as I lifted the first blue suit jacket from its hanger, I began to cry. I cried and cried as we pulled his clothing from the closet and bureau and filled one plastic bag after another. When Fatima told me she would be giving David's clothes to her family and others who could use them, I felt a little better.

And then I picked up one of his favorite shirts. It had been one of my father's favorite summer shirts, from Brooks Brothers, pink cotton checked, smooth, and expensive I am sure. Dad always sought the best tailored clothes. I imagined my dad on holiday or on a hot midsummer Minnesota evening on my parents' screened porch, a martini in hand, happy wearing this beautiful pink shirt. He would be telling a joke or some self-deprecating story about himself. After my father's death I took the pink checked shirt for David. I'd known he would love it, and he did.

He wore it on hot London evenings and special evenings ashore when we were sailing on *Bellatrix*. Whenever David put it on, I knew he felt good, lighthearted, anticipating a joyous evening. David's shoulders were broader than my father's so every now and then I had to mend a torn seam on the sleeve with a tiny needle, careful not to poke too large a hole in fabric that had become smooth and worn with age. I washed the shirt at home, and Fatima ironed it and folded it onto his shirt shelf.

And the blue striped shirt, the button-down that I could swear he was wearing the night in 1978 when we first met. He had rolled up the sleeves. Fatima smiled down at me sitting on the floor holding his shirt. She had turned the collar several times.

"Shall we do the sweaters?" she asked gently.

I stood up and reached into the closet. There was the white cotton Greek sweater. One summer afternoon we visited Paxos, the small island south of Corfu. On the waterfront was a row of lovely classical buildings interspersed with small stalls owned by vendors selling their homemade wares. And as we approached, David put the motor into reverse to go "stern to" the quay. We secured *Bellatrix* and found a little cafe for lunch. Then we did some shopping and returned to the boat. David started the motor, and, as he did, a stream of black oil shot out of the exhaust pipe directly onto a linen and cotton stall, and the blast sprayed a white cotton sweater. The vendor rushed towards us waving his arms and screaming at the top of his lungs, "Politzio, Politzio." and instantly the police arrived. Naturally they took their countryman's position. So David dug into his pockets to recompense the vendor and claim the damaged goods. Later I washed the oil out of the sweater that David wore until his death. That sweater I could not give away.

And then there was the Canadian wool plaid lumber jacket that he wore sailing in rough sea weather. A business friend had given it to David, who loved the bold tan and bright green and relished the warmth of heavy wool. I think the jacket reminded him of his mother's Canadian heritage, and he wore it all year long, in England on brisk, rainy sailing days on the Solent and as protection against strong European winds, Mediterranean mistrals, and Ionian meltamies. To me that jacket symbolized security, riding out the storm to home port. It was David in this jacket that best emblemized his strong presence, the fact that he was a man who knew what he was doing, took charge, and always brought his crew safely home. That jacket also symbolized his success in the insurance business, the confidence he gave his cohorts and customers. He called himself a "man of the people," and he liked to recall his Cornish heritage as well as his Canadian roots. That jacket wove the many fibers of his life together.

It was another item of clothing I could never give away.

In a bureau drawer I found the navy blue t-shirt that David had worn under his sailing shirts on cold Solent days. Later he gave it to me to wear to bed, to cover my shoulders; we never wore pajamas. I pressed the tee shirt to my chest, then placed it on the bed. It would join the shirts, the jacket, and the sweater that I was taking with me to Minnesota, where I would keep them in a special box to cherish.

There, I had said it. I was going to Minnesota. Then and there, sitting on the floor of our bedroom surrounded by black plastic bags, Fatima hovering over me, I made the decision. Our task complete, I helped Fatima tie up the bags, and without my having said a word, she understood that the items I had placed on the bed ought not to be touched. She may have understood I would soon be leaving; she sensed from time to time my homesickness.

But she didn't say that. She only smiled and gave me a hug as she hoisted the bags and opened the front door.

Within days, with fresh energy, I moved into high gear, contacting a real estate agent and meeting with my stepdaughters, Bino, Niotti, and Talia, and other close family and friends to tell them of my decision, and though I knew I faced weeks of sorting and packing and making decisions about possessions, what would stay with the girls and what would come with me, I suddenly had the energy for that. I would take half of his scrapbooks, those dating from our marriage, a few special paintings, and my personal belongings. All the rest was David's, which he had designated before his death as gifts to his children and grandchildren.

As we packed together, David's family and I, we felt sad but we remained cheerful. I promised them I would return each year to visit, that I would stay in touch, remain close, just as David would wish. We understood each other. They had their young, active lives in London, and I had my roots to rediscover in Minnesota, and those leafy branches stretching to Charlie and Juli in Portland, Chris and Lisa in Petaluma, and Michael in Los Angeles.

And so it was on January 31, 2003, I returned to what would again become my home, and a brand-new chapter, another scrapbook to begin, to design each page to meld memories of London with fresh accounts of family reunions on the West Coast, activities that I would explore and embrace in my own community, always arranged as David had taught me, with thought and theme.